THE DREAM

"The dream is always the same. This long hallway. The keys. The doors. Searching for him."

"Who?"

How can I explain it? I didn't even know it until just then. That the guy in that theater—the face I finally got to see after all these years—is the love of my life. I'm sixteen. I know that sounds crazy. Not to mention he only exists in my dreams. Instead, I mumble, "I don't know."

Dr. Koios nods. "Well, I'll tell you what. Let's try again next week. Same time. We'll see if we can't conquer these nightmares together. Until then, don't do anything differently. Let's wait to use the technique in my office, where I'm sure you're safe and I can guide you. All right?"

His face is kindly, and I find myself nodding.

But really, inside I'm dying a little. Because all I can think about is getting back to Sebastian.

Finally. A name. And a face. To go with the voice of the man of my dreams.

OTHER BOOKS YOU MAY ENJOY

IN
DREAMS

ERICA ORLOFF

speak

An Imprint of Penguin Group (USA)

SPEAK
Published by the Penguin Group
Penguin Group (USA) LLC
375 Hudson Street
New York, New York 10014

USA • Canada • UK • Ireland • Australia
New Zealand • India • South Africa • China

penguin.com
A Penguin Random House Company

First published in the United States of America by Speak,
an imprint of Penguin Group (USA) LLC, 2014

LIBRARY OF CONGRESS CATALOGING-IN-PUBLICATION DATA IS AVAILABLE

Speak ISBN 978-0-14-242407-0

Printed in the United States of America

1 3 5 7 9 10 8 6 4 2

To Alexa, Nicholas, Isabella, and Jack
And to sweet Zaid

ACKNOWLEDGMENTS

An enormous thank you to my supportive editor, Jennifer Bonnell, who is a dream to work with.

Thank you to my agent, Jay Poynor, for loving the concept.

To Charlie Long, a great writer and critique partner, who catches my many gaffes. Our coffee-fueled sessions have meant a lot to me.

To the usual suspects, you know who you are.

To Pam Morrell, Marybeth Johnson, G. L. Yates, and Barb "B. B." Bingham, for everything you have done for me this last year especially as I fought a hard battle. I am so blessed to have such amazing women in my life. Like Aphrodite in this book, you rock.

A thank you to Trudy Hale and the Porches writing retreat, a place where I can unplug and write to my heart's content.

And finally, to my children, Alexa, Nick, Bella, and Jack the Pirate Boy. I love you to the ends of the earth, to the world of dreams and back.

IN
DREAMS

O sleep, O gentle sleep,
Nature's soft nurse, how have I frighted thee,
That thou no more wilt weigh my eyelids down
And steep my senses in forgetfulness?

WILLIAM SHAKESPEARE, *HENRY IV, PART II*

Dreams are true while they last,
and do we not live in dreams?
ALFRED, LORD TENNYSON

The dream remains the same.
I am searching for him. I walk, terrified, down a long, dark hallway of many doors. I hear every shallow, agonizing breath I take. I hear my own heart crashing against my rib cage. He needs me. My mouth is dry, acid burning my throat. In my dream, I have a large circular brass key ring, and hundreds of elegant, intricate old-fashioned keys clank and rattle with each step. Each key opens a lock on one of the myriad doors. Some doors are tall, and some are so short I would have to duck to enter them. Some are wooden and heavy. Some are painted red or black or the color of the sky. And behind each door is its own universe, each one unique. Some are beautiful, achingly so, worlds I never want to leave.

Some are as dark as a coffin. The dark ones frighten me so much I fear dying. In my dreams, I am always longing for him.

I never find him.

Tonight is no different. I wake up, soaked with sweat, and sit up in my bed. The light is already on. It is always on, because I wake from my dreams and nightmares so upset, heart thumping in my chest, that I crave the light. I'm sixteen and still afraid of the dark.

My cat stares at me from the foot of my bed, his yellow-green eyes enigmatic. He rolls over to have his belly scratched.

"No, Puck," I whisper, rubbing my fingers through his calico fur. "I didn't find him."

I grab my dream notebook from my nightstand and scribble what I remember.

The room was black and steamy, kudzu hanging from trees. A swampy bayou with murky water, a strong oily smell. And I was pushing away vines from my face. My hair was in tangles. The vines stung me, scratching my cheeks and neck. I couldn't really see. All of a sudden, roots began grabbing my legs, twirling and growing around them, and pulling

me into the mud. They had sharp thorns, like pins pricking me. I screamed and tore at the vines until my fingers bled and I could escape. The whole time, I could hear him calling me. "Iris! Iris!" He sounded desperate.

∞

And then I woke up. My dream is always of that corridor, of the doors and the ring of keys, and the world behind each door. But since I was thirteen or so, it has also been about that *voice*. I don't know who calls me in my dreams. I just know it's *him*—the same voice every time, even if it changes somehow. I know that doesn't make sense. But sometimes he sounds as if he's in pain. Sometimes he's laughing and asking me to come find him. His voice is gravelly—almost a growl when he is upset. Soft like the wind through the oak tree outside my bedroom window when he is comforting me. I love his voice. Sometimes, I think I hear it in my head. Like the whisper of my heart's desire. It is the voice of the person I know I am meant to be with. I just wish I knew to whom it belonged.

I glance at my alarm clock. Two A.M. Terrific. I have a trig exam tomorrow, and once again, I am the insomniac girl. My best friend, Annie, calls me that— says I am the girl who never sleeps. Lucky for me, she drinks enough Diet Coke, Starbucks venti Caramel Macchiatos, and Red Bull that she's also up most nights. We text and video-chat at crazy hours. And half the time she's sleeping over here or me there. But even if we're not under the same roof, I know I can call her if I am afraid after a nightmare.

But tonight, instead, I slip out of bed and listen at the door. I don't hear a sound. Or rather I hear the sounds of a sleeping house, the slight rattle of our heater, the refrigerator motor, a couple of creaks. I open my bedroom door and peer down the hall. Grandpa's bedroom is shut, no light streaming out from under the door. He's usually on the computer till all hours, looking for a cure for my mother.

I tiptoe down to her room and open the door. The room is dark and cool, the blinds shut tight, curtains drawn, a small night-light in the corner. We play an iPod of her favorite classical music very, very softly. Claude Debussy's *Nocturnes*. I hope it helps her dream peacefully. Her room smells of lavender—we keep a plant of it on her windowsill. Grandpa and I read somewhere that it is good for sleep.

My mother has Sleeping Beauty syndrome. Despite the fairy-tale name, it's a real disorder. She sleeps for months on end, sometimes awake for only a few hours a week. Hers is the most severe case on record.

She sleeps the longest, the deepest, and the last few years has come back to the land of the awake for less and less time. Sometimes, we have to feed her through IVs because she doesn't even wake to eat and starts wasting away. The doctors have scanned her brain so many times, always searching for something in the pictures that could explain it. But they have no explanation. It's an orphan disease, meaning a disease so rare there is little funding to find a cure. Three years ago, my mother said she was tired of being poked and prodded. She doesn't want to see any more doctors about it.

She looks so peaceful.

An antique bentwood rocking chair that belonged to my grandmother and her mother before her is next to the bed. Most nights, Grandpa and I take turns sitting in it, and we talk to my mom. Sometimes Grandpa dozes in it. Tonight I flick on the soft light on her dresser, which is also an antique and has a matching mirror. Then I sit down in the rocker and take her hand. Her fingers are long and elegant like a piano player's. Tonight her hand is chilly.

"Hi, Mom," I whisper. "I got an A-plus on my English paper, the one on Shakespeare. Which sort of makes up for the C in trig. Right? I think Annie's going to sleep over this weekend. We're going to rent some movies. She's going through a major Ryan Gosling phase. Even if we go to her house, Grandpa will be here with you. He said he'd call me if you wake up. . . . I'm thinking of cutting my hair." I turn to look in the mirror. My hair is long and black and curly. And unruly. If I try to blow it out straight and flat-iron it, the process takes over an hour. So I mostly let it curl. It reaches the middle of my back, and I've always been afraid to cut it, worried I'll look like a poodle. "Maybe not. Maybe I'll just leave it. I know . . . I always leave it, right? Oh, Annie made the all-county soccer team. And tonight I had a bad dream."

Her eyelids flutter, at what I guess is a flicker of a dream floating past.

"It's the same dream, Mom. I wish I knew what it means." Sometimes I feel as if I'm crazy. Sixteen years old, and I swear I've been having these dreams since forever. At least since I can remember dreaming. Who is the man I'm searching for? "I don't get it. Why can't I dream of flying or . . . I don't know . . . Annie dreams her teeth fall out. I mean, why can't I have normal dreams? Why can't I sleep?"

She doesn't answer. She never does. I stand and get her hairbrush, and I brush her hair, then splay it across her pillow. It's a rich chestnut color. She really does look like Sleeping Beauty.

"Good night, Mommy," I whisper. I look at the picture of the two of us on her nightstand taken shortly after I was born. Taped to her dresser mirror is my second-grade school picture—the year I was missing my two front teeth—and another one of the two of us on top of the Empire State Building. I've never met my father. My mother said she was artificially inseminated. My grandfather once said it was "complicated." All my life it's just been me and her, and Grandpa.

I turn off the light and listen to her breathe. Then I leave and return to my bedroom, positive I will be up until the delicate fingers of pink dawn stretch across the sky.

I pull the sheets back to climb into bed, and push Puck over to one side.

"What the . . . ?"

Little specks of blood are flicked across my sheets like a Jackson Pollock painting—the guy who dripped paint. It's only then that I look down at my ankles and see it—a raw, red mark on my right leg. In the shape of a vine, wrapped around my ankle. And little pinpricks of blood. Just like in my nightmare.

I sit down on my bed, and my teeth start to chatter. I tell myself this can't be true. That there is some explanation. Some condition, some way that the impossible is possible. I look at my ankle again in the light. I am not imagining it.

My nightmare is *real*.

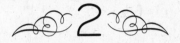

2

We are such stuff
As dreams are made on, and our little life
Is rounded with a sleep.

WILLIAM SHAKESPEARE, *THE TEMPEST*

"I have the solution to your problem," Annie says, flopping onto her bed. I haven't told her about the blood or the mark on my ankle . . . because really? I'd sound so crazy.

"What? My trig grade? I just don't understand Mr. Blake. He never *explains* anything. Whenever I ask a question, he just explains it the same exact way as the first time. Which, if I had understood, would mean I didn't have a question. Or a C."

"No, not Mr. Blake. Your insomnia. Your bad dreams."

"Annie . . . come on. You know I've tried *everything*. Acupuncture, sleeping pills even—which didn't work except to make me a zombie the next day. Lavender.

Some concoction from the health food store that Dr. Oz swears by. I'm telling you, nothing works. It's hopeless."

"What about hypnosis?"

"A hypnotist?"

"No. A *hypnotherapist*."

"I don't know. Sounds weird. Even for you."

"Look at this article," she says, shoving a magazine under my nose. "My mom showed it to me."

Annie's mom is one of those women who mothers the entire world. The Caseys have six kids of their own, including a set of four-year-old twin boys we call the Tiny Terrors. And there are always, it seems, a dozen kids over all the time—playing in the backyard, or sleeping over, or doing whatever. They have a big old Victorian-style house, and during the winter when the leaves are off the trees, you can even glimpse the Hudson River from Annie's bedroom window.

I read the article in some women's magazine—the kind at the supermarket checkout that promises "the secret to wash away belly fat" and "antiaging secrets." The hypnotherapist quoted in the article is from a town in New Jersey not far from where we live in Nyack, New York.

"What if he hypnotizes me and, I don't know, tells me to get naked or something?"

"It doesn't work that way. Read the box there." She points to the bottom of page 34.

I read it. It doesn't *sound* as if he can hypnotize me to take off all my clothes. But still. "Maybe. I'll think about it."

Annie looks at me. "You've got to try something. You can't go on forever like this. Maybe your subconscious is telling you something. Maybe that's why you can't sleep."

"I don't know. Like what?"

She shrugs. "My dad says he thinks it's because you have a lot of responsibility. Way more than most kids our age. Your grandpa is getting way up there, and your mom—"

"Grandpa's only seventy-seven."

"I rest my case. Love your grandpa—and love, love, *love* his souvlaki—but he's beyond ancient."

"Oh come on, Annie. He beats the crap out of us in Texas hold 'em. His mind is still totally all there. He still lifts weights at the gym. I think he may even have a girlfriend."

"Get out!"

I smile. "Yeah. I see them at the gym. There's this

one woman. He always heads to the treadmill next to hers, and they talk the whole time. And she looks, like . . . I don't know. Fifty. She can still rock leggings and a sports bra."

"A younger babe. Good for Grandpa. But still, my dad says it's too much stress for you. When was the last time your mom was even awake?"

"A week ago. She woke up for an hour or so. She drank about four of the chocolate protein shakes that we made her. We talked a little. Then she went back to sleep."

"All right. Let's go at this from a different angle." Annie furrowed her brow. "What do you know about this mystery man in the dream?"

"Not much. I don't know his name. Or what he looks like. I only know his voice. It's the sexiest voice I've ever heard—and completely unique. And I know I'm meant to meet him. I have dreamed of him hundreds of times. Maybe thousands."

"Maybe he's your soul mate."

"Maybe. I just want to see his face, Annie. I wish I could explain it. In my dreams, I *have* to find him—like it's a matter of life or death."

"Or love. Think of what Carl Jung would say!"

Annie and I have stacks of dream interpretation books and encyclopedias. It's become sort of a hobby. Like if you dream you're flying, it's supposed to mean you are in control of your life or a situation. And Carl Jung, who believed in dream symbols, said there was an archetype of soul mates. He said we each have a male part of us and a female part, and that sometimes there are "divine couples" who fit together perfectly. Some people search their whole lives for their other half. Then again, Carl Jung had an open marriage, so I'm not so sure he knew what he was talking about.

"Annie, I don't know what the voice means. I just want to be able to go out without piling on concealer under my eyes. I would give just about anything to sleep through the night."

In fact, in all my life, I have never slept more than four hours in a row. My record without sleep is thirty-nine hours. I toss. I turn. I've tried different pillows. My grandfather has bought me four different mattresses. Including that one with space technology that's supposed to be the greatest mattress ever made. It may well be, and maybe astronauts sleep on the thing, but it still didn't do the trick for me.

"Well, I honestly think you should try the hypnotherapist."

I still think he might hypnotize me to do something weird. "Would you go with me?"

Annie rolls her eyes. "Like you have to ask."

I look down at the magazine again. "What do I have to lose?"

∽

If Wikipedia had a picture of a typical therapist, Dr. Koios would be it. He wears a tan tweed jacket with corduroy patches on the elbows, and his gray beard is clipped short. He has horn-rimmed glasses and pale, kind eyes. He sort of looks like Sigmund Freud—one of Carl Jung's contemporaries. I tell him my whole story and background—my mom and her sleep disease and the fact that I have had insomnia my whole life. As I talk he keeps repeating, "Very interesting," while tapping his two index fingers together. All that's missing is his smoking a pipe.

Then he explains his whole hypnotic process to Annie and me. After telling us it's really about deep, deep relaxation, he says, "What I am actually going to be doing, Iris, is teaching you how to hypnotize yourself, ultimately, so you can relax into sleep when you're home. I'm also going to give you a trigger. When you go home tonight, and it's time for bed, you are going to use this trigger, which should take you back to the relaxed state and then allow you to fall asleep peacefully. The trigger needs to be something you're comfortable with."

Like what?"

"Well, some people, before they go to sleep, might stroke a soft blanket. Or they might even have a stuffed animal or something that they hold. And then what I do is transfer the feelings you'll have when you are relaxed and in a hypnotic state onto that object or trigger."

"I have a quilt on my bed, and the border on it is green velvet and super soft. I guess I could use that."

"Excellent. Now, before we begin, do you have any questions?"

"Not really." I'm sitting in a big, comfy armchair. My feet are propped up on an ottoman, and I see the mark on my ankle. I didn't tell him about that. Because I really don't need some therapist thinking I'm crazy. It's bad enough *I* think I'm nuts.

"All right then," he says in a soothing voice. "First, sink into the chair. Feel your body getting heavier and heavier. . . . Now focus on your breath. With each inhale, you sink deeper into relaxation; with each exhale, you sink still deeper. Breathe. Breathe. In and out, relaxing deeper and deeper."

Minutes pass, and I hear his voice droning on as if it's down a tunnel. My body relaxes, and I even feel a little sleepy. My limbs are heavy. But then just as I finally start to let go, to drift into a place where I just might fall asleep, I'm in the long hallway, the one with many doors.

My heart starts beating faster. I can still hear Dr. Koios's voice saying, "Inhale, exhale," but I also hear *him*, the man in my dreams. He's calling me.

"Iris! Iris!"

I fumble for my keys, hands shaking. There are so many keys, how can I be sure of the right one? But somehow I instinctively know. This one. I select a beautiful brass key—and open a tall, heavy wooden door with a polished brass knob so shiny I can see my reflection in it. I have to lean my shoulder into the door and push with all my weight to get it to open. And when I step into the room on the other side, I'm in the back of a large fancy theater—like on Broadway. No one is in there, and it's very dark, and the silence is stifling. And creepy.

The seats are rich royal purple velvet with polished mahogany armrests. I walk down the sloped aisle, my footsteps muffled by the carpet, hearing myself breathe. My teeth chatter—the theater is icy cold. When I exhale, I can see my breath. And as I walk, the curtains part with a near-silent whoosh. A man is standing on the stage, directly in the center, in the brilliant beam of a spotlight. My stomach drops. It's him. I know it is, even though his back is to me. His hair is long—to his shoulders—and dark. And then he turns around. My knees wobble, and my stomach flip-flops. I finally see him. He's my age. And he is . . . beautiful. I have never seen a guy so hot in my entire life. And then he smiles, and he has two deep dimples, and dark eyes that seem to laugh. And he says, "Iris! You found me." He starts toward the front of the stage, a look of desperation on his face—desperation and happiness.

I start running down the sloping aisle, feeling this joy that I have never felt before, but before I can get to him, before I reach the stage, before I can finally touch him and have him hold me in his arms, behind me I hear someone banging on the door to the theater. Loudly. Urgently. Angrily.

"You can't let them take you away from me," he begs. His face is horrified.

"Who are you?" I ask, trying to run to him, but my legs are suddenly heavy.

"Sebastian. My name is Sebastian. I want to go with you, Iris," he begs in that growly voice of his.

"How?" I ask him, but I hear people behind me, charging up the aisle. I'm afraid to look. But finally, I turn my head, and I see them. Storming toward me.

Men in dark suits, wearing dark, mirrored glasses. Men with the lean yet well-built muscles of former soldiers, who look like a private security detail for someone famous or very important. Stone-faced, with grim mouths. I turn to look at Sebastian on the stage, but he's being pulled away, too, behind the curtains, by more of these efficient, military-like men. It takes five of them to hold him because he is fighting them so fiercely, and I feel them on me— these men—grabbing my legs and pulling me away. "No!" I scream.

"Iris! Iris!" He calls for me.

And then it is Dr. Koios's voice I hear. "Iris . . . Iris . . . open your eyes."

I don't want to. I shake my head from side to side. I want to be back in that place with *him*. I've waited years to see him. And I have questions about who he is and why he's always in my dreams. But Dr. Koios's voice insists.

"Iris, you need to come back now."

Finally, I open my eyes and blink a few times. Dr. Koios is standing over me, a concerned look on his face.

"You were in distress. Are you okay?"

I nod.

"Iris, can you tell me where you were? You were relaxing. I could see you going into a hypnotic state, but then you were obviously very upset, thrashing in the chair."

I gaze up at him. "I don't know. The dream is always the same. This long hallway. The keys. The doors. Searching for him."

"Who?"

How can I explain it? I didn't even know it until just then. That the guy in that theater—the face I finally got to see after all these years—is the love of my life. I'm sixteen. I know that sounds crazy. Not to mention he only exists in my dreams. Instead, I mumble, "I don't know."

Dr. Koios nods. "Well, I'll tell you what. Let's try again next week. Same time. We'll see if we can't conquer these nightmares together. Until then, don't do anything differently. Let's wait to use the technique in my office, where I'm sure you're safe and I can guide you. All right?"

His face is kindly, and I find myself nodding.

But really, inside I'm dying a little. Because all I can think about is getting back to Sebastian.

Finally. A name. And a face. To go with the voice of the man of my dreams.

3

I dream, therefore I exist.

AUGUST STRINDBERG, *A MADMAN'S DEFENSE*

On the way home in Annie's cute little yellow VW bug, I'm quiet.

"So what happened?" she asks me. "Did you get hypnotized?"

"Yeah. Sort of. I felt myself going deeper and deeper under. Like I was finally going to *sleep*. And then . . . and then I was in this weird dream. And I finally saw him."

"Who?"

"The guy in my dream."

"Oh my God! *Get out!* So do you know him? Is he a movie star? Someone from school?"

"No. But he has a name: Sebastian."

"And you're sure you've never seen him before?"

"Trust me. *This guy* I would remember. Oh my *God*, but I would remember."

"So now what?"

I shrug. "I don't know. Dr. Koios couldn't get me to fall asleep for real. I was relaxing, and then all of a sudden, I was in my nightmare again. In that strange world, the long hallway. Like half in a dream, and half hypnotized. So maybe he can't help me after all."

"Well, this was just the first session. Maybe you have to get hypnotized a few times for it really to work."

I sigh. "I don't know. I made another appointment, though."

She pulls off the highway, and we head down Main Street in our town, which is lined with cafés and restaurants and cute shops, a yoga studio. My breath catches. I see them. Two of the men from the nightmare. They're standing on the corner outside a bakery.

"Annie." I swallow. "Tell me you see those two guys there." I whisper the words so quietly I can barely hear myself.

"The two *Men in Black*–looking guys?"

"Yes," I exhale, slightly relieved. Because if she didn't see them, then I would be certifiable. But now

I don't know which is worse. Because that means my dream world is real. Like the marks on my leg. And that's impossible. I feel as if I'm going to throw up.

"Kind of weird-looking," she says. "What are they, Secret Service or something? Is, like, the president coming here?" We stop at a red light, and the two of them are staring at us. At least I think they are behind their mirrored sunglasses.

"Yeah, I guess. Just step on it when the light changes, okay?"

"Sure." She looks over at me. "Iris, babe, you're pale as a ghost. Are you sure you're okay?"

"Not really."

The light changes, and she floors it up Main Street. In the side-view mirror, I see the two men in the dark suits turn to look in our direction as we speed away. I feel icy cold. My stomach clenches.

Annie drives to my street, pulls in front of my house, and parks the car. "All right, spill it. I know something's wrong, and it's not just that you can't sleep. I can tell. What is it? I'm your bestie. You have to tell me. It's, like, the law."

I wait a minute. Finally, I pull up the leg of my jeans and show her the marks.

"What does this look like to you?"

"I don't know. Like your leg got attacked by a rosebush or something."

I am not imagining it. She sees the marks, too. I tell her about the drops of blood on my bed. About the dreams.

"And those two guys? They were in my dream. It's like they followed me back here."

"You do know that's impossible, right?"

"Completely. But that doesn't mean they weren't there. You saw them. I didn't make them up. And it doesn't mean I don't have vine burn on my ankle."

She leans over and stares at the marks—there is the imprint of a thorn and a leaf, perfectly shaped, on my leg in scarlet, and the imprints of leaves and vines completely encircle my leg at the ankle. Suddenly, Annie slaps my knee. "Maybe you have the stigmata!"

"The *what*?"

"You know. The stigmata! We only go to church on Christmas and Easter. But you've seen devil horror movies, right? It's like when someone gets marks on them—"

"Annie, first of all, I'm not Catholic. Second, I don't have marks on my *palms*! I have them on my ankle. And men in suits? Where does that come into your little devil movie? I'm not possessed."

"All right. I was just trying to think of a logical explanation."

"You call that logical?"

"Well, how do you explain it then?"

"That's the thing, I can't." I open the car door and climb out. "But I'm not crazy."

"Puh-leeze. I've known you forever. I know you're not. Or if you are, then so am I. Call me later, okay?"

"Okay. Call you after dinner."

I shut the car door and walk into the house.

"Grandpa?" I call out, but he doesn't answer. I poke my head in his bedroom, but he isn't there. And then I see it. His computer. It's on, but the monitor is asleep.

My grandfather spends every waking moment on that thing. He tells me he's searching for a cure for Mom. I sit down at his desk and hit the mouse. The screen comes on again, but instead of searching for Sleeping Beauty syndrome, I see he's researching Greek mythology. I click History for the drop-down menu. That's *all* he's researching, according to what I can see.

Weird. Nothing about drugs, doctors, or specialists.

I feel kind of guilty, as if I'm spying on him. I get up and go into Mom's room. She's sleeping, but I see she's upset. She's kicking her legs and turning her head from side to side. Sometimes she does this just before she wakes up. I go to her bedside. Grandpa and I like to be there when she wakes in case she's confused.

And then I hear her call my name. "Iris!"

"Mom," I soothe. "I'm here." Her forehead is drenched, and she's hot to the touch.

But she doesn't wake up.

And then she kicks at the sheets again. She opens her mouth. Only this time she doesn't call for me.

She shouts a different name instead.

"Sebastian!"

*As everyone knows, the ancients before Aristotle
did not consider the dream a product of the
dreaming mind, but a divine inspiration . . .*

SIGMUND FREUD

If my life were a movie, right now my mom would
wake up. But she doesn't. She tosses her head back
and forth a few times, and then she seems to recede
into her deep slumber, far from me, far from the real
world. I wipe her forehead with a washcloth and kiss
her cheek. It won't do me any good to try to wake her
up. I know from experience. If you wake someone
with Kleine-Levin syndrome—the fancy name for
Sleeping Beauty syndrome—they're still out of it. It's
a little like talking to someone who's really drunk.
I've tried before, and she's not coherent.

I watch her sleep for a few minutes, trying to make
my head stop hurting. Wanting things to be normal.
Even if my normal isn't like anyone else's. Even if

my mom sleeps her life away. I want things to make sense. *Sebastian*. It's not a typical name. In fact, I've never met anyone with that name ever. How? That's all I keep thinking. How did the vine marks get on my leg? How did the military-type men from my dream end up on a street corner in my hometown? How did my mother call out the name of the man of my dreams when I didn't even know his name until that afternoon when I was hypnotized?

I want to pretend none of this ever happened. I leave her room and go to the kitchen to make myself something to eat. I hear Grandpa's car in the driveway—he drives a cute BMW convertible, and when I graduate from high school, he has promised it to me as my graduation present.

He comes through the front door and makes his way to the kitchen, where I'm trying to choose between four different boxes of cereal, trying to pretend today was like any other day.

"Gourmet dining, I see," he says. "Shall I light candles and break out the good china?"

I worry my voice will sound shaky. But I try to joke with him like I always do. "Dinner of champions. Frosted Flakes? Corn Pops? Lucky Charms? Or Raisin Bran? Or we could get really adventurous and go for Pop-Tarts."

"How about takeout?"

"Okay," I say, and open our take-out drawer. My grandmother died of cancer when I was six months old. Apparently, she was a great Italian cook—Sicilian, actually, but then she learned to make the Greek food my grandfather loves. That cooking gene skipped my mom—badly. And it most definitely skipped me. Grandpa can make three things: mac and cheese from the blue box, grilled souvlaki on the barbecue, and tuna-fish sandwiches with minced pickles in them—sounds gross, but they're delicious. Anything beyond that repertoire means takeout—and we have menus for every pizza parlor, sub shop, Chinese place, and sushi restaurant within a ten-mile radius of our house.

I pick up about a dozen menus, spread them out, and jokingly fan my face, grateful that he's here and that he looks and is acting completely and totally like my grandfather. "What are you in the mood for, Grandpa?"

"Ah, take-out roulette. Well, being as I just got home, how about the Chinese place that delivers? That way I don't have to go out again. Order me the Szechuan pork—extra hot. Two egg rolls. And shrimp wontons."

I take my phone from my back pocket and find the

restaurant in my contacts—we order so often, every place is in there, and they all know my voice. I order his food and then mine—shrimp with snow peas. Then we go into the living room and wait. I try to act as if everything is okay. But I picture my mom's mouth forming the word *Sebastian*. I didn't imagine it. I shut my eyes tight and open them again. This is my living room. Everything is how it always is, right down to the thick, glossy art books stacked just so on the coffee table. I try to forget today. Maybe I really am just overtired. Delusional. Except I know I'm not.

"How have you been sleeping?" he asks.

I shrug. "Okay. I mean . . . you know, not sleeping. So nothing's changed."

"And to think we spent two thousand dollars on that fancy mattress."

"I know."

"And how was the hypnotherapist?"

"Actually, he says he can help me. I made another appointment."

"Good. That's very good, Lambie."

Yeah. His nickname for me. His little lamb. Annie abuses it and calls me Mutton.

He picks up the *New York Times* we get delivered

every day. I pick up my book. We don't have a television in our living room. Or in the den. In fact, I have one in my bedroom only because I begged for it so I wouldn't be the only freak at school without. My mother, before she got sick, and my grandfather are really into reading, learning, visiting museums. Even with my mom sick, Grandpa and I usually have a standing date twice a month to visit an art museum, or attend a lecture, or see a Broadway play, or something. Annie usually comes. Her parents love that she's getting all kinds of culture. And it's kind of weird, but with the exception of trig, all that reading and museums mean I don't have to try too hard to get straight As.

I keep glancing over at him while I pretend to read. I want to ask him questions. I really do. Like how my mom called out Sebastian, the exact name of the guy who has been part of my dreams for years. I want to tell him about the marks on my ankle. But I don't want to worry him. He has enough to worry about with my mom. He doesn't need to start with me, too.

I think he feels me staring at him, but all I see is his white hair over the *Times*. Then he lowers the paper. I just smile at him and then look down at my book. We sit like that, me curled on the couch, and him reclining in his La-Z-Boy, until the doorbell rings.

He stands, reaches into his back pocket, takes out his wallet, and hands me two twenties and a ten. "Not sure of the total," he says.

I open the door, and a man is standing there holding a brown paper bag with our Chinese food. Only it's not Cheung, the son of the owner of Ming's Palace. It's a guy with dark sunglasses, a black T-shirt, jeans, and biceps the size of small tree trunks. On his forearm is a tattoo of an intricate serpent. And something about the tattoo looks familiar, as if I've seen it somewhere. Total déjà vu. Maybe in a dream? My throat goes dry. Something about this feels fifty shades of wrong.

I glance back at Grandpa, fear in my eyes. Grandpa climbs out of his chair and steps closer to me.

I turn to look at the deliveryman, and I manage to whisper, "How much?"

With one hand still holding the bag, he uses his other hand to whip off his sunglasses. And where his eyes should be are . . . mirrors. Or glass. I can't quite tell. I want to look away, to run away, but I can't stop staring into them, and I see swirls of black storm clouds. And lightning. His eyes, they're mesmerizing. He grins. More of a leer that makes my throat feel even tighter.

Finally, I tear my gaze away, and I look behind him. Near our big oak tree—the oak tree with my old tree house still in it—is a dog. A mean, snarling, snapping dog.

Then the dog bolts a few yards toward our door, growling so loud it's an earth-shaking rumble, and I literally gasp. It has three heads. *Cerberus*. My heart pounds, and I'm frozen.

I know I called Ming's Palace. I can smell Chinese food. I know this is real, but I swear it is a dream.

I slam the door shut—or try to—but the delivery guy manages to block me with one shove of his supersize arm. I look at the tattoo, and the snake is moving—actually moving on his skin, twisting and slithering, its scales shiny and black.

"What? No tip?" His voice drips with menace.

"Grandpa!" I shriek. I back up into our living room, but the guy is coming after me, barging inside, and behind him on the front steps the dog is growling. Out of the corner of my eye, I see Grandpa has grabbed his prized bat—his Yankees bat signed by Don Mattingly, the possession he loves most in the world—off the mantel of the fireplace.

The man with the strange eyes keeps coming toward me. He drops our Chinese food on the floor and knocks over a lamp, which shatters into a thousand pieces. The lightbulb pops and sparks, and half the room is now dim.

Grandpa swings the bat, hard, and connects. It splinters against the man's arm, and still the man with the strange eyes keeps coming, kicking the ottoman aside and then knocking the coffee table over so he can get to me. I skitter over furniture and back up until I am against the wall. Grandpa searches the living room. I can see him moving toward the fireplace and the iron tongs.

The man looms over me, blocking my view of anything but his face. "What do you want?" I ask. My throat is so paralyzed with terror, the words come out in a croak.

"Stay away, Iris." He emphasizes the *s* in my name like the hiss of a snake. The man's voice is cold. The voice of a killer, devoid of warmth or humanity.

He knows my name. I feel the wall at my back, which tells me this is really happening, the plaster cool to my touch. There is nowhere to run. I can't breathe I am so scared. "Stay away from what?" From where? From who? My mind races, but it's taking all of me just to keep breathing.

"You don't belong. You shouldn't exist. Stay out of the Underworld."

"The what?" He's not making any sense. Not that anything today has.

He leans in close to me, until I feel his lips pressed against my ear. They are moist, and I know I am not dreaming. He's real. This is happening. "The Underworld. You know. Deep down. *You've always known*. Keep away."

I move my face and glance to my left, and I see Grandpa raise the tongs high in the air. But before he can bring them down on the man's head, the man whirls around. With one hand, he grabs Grandpa's wrist tight. My grandfather drops to his knees and his face pales, then turns florid. I scream—a pitch so high and frightened and loud I didn't know I had it in me.

"Grandpa!"

I tug on the man's arm. "Don't hurt him! I'll do whatever you ask. Just please don't hurt him." I hear how desperately I am begging. How scared I am.

And then the man lets go. He whirls and grabs my face in his left hand, pressing his fingers into my cheeks until it hurts so bad tears stream down my face. "Remember . . . stay away." Then he releases me and storms out of the house, slamming the door.

I run to the window. He whistles for his dog.

His three-headed beast of a dog. And the two of them start down the street, then disappear into a shroud of fog that has suddenly appeared from out of nowhere.

5

In dreams no man wears a mask.

EDWARD COUNSEL

Iris, are you okay?" Grandpa asks shakily.

I nod, not trusting my voice. Grandpa and I survey the mess. It's almost comforting that things are broken—that way I know it all actually happened. That I didn't imagine the whole thing. That I didn't imagine the man. Or his beast.

"Come on, let's deal with this later," he says, and wraps an arm around my shoulders, leading me into the kitchen. I lean my head on him, grateful for the scent of his Polo aftershave. For normal.

I touch my back pocket, thinking we should call 911. But what would I say? Our Chinese food was delivered by a man with mirror eyes and a three-headed dog?

"We need to do something," I urge Grandpa. What, I have no idea. I guess I expect him to have the answers.

"We'll talk."

Talk?

I stare at him, but it's clear he just wants us to sit down. Like he has to collect himself. But most of all, I notice that he doesn't seem shocked. As for me, my stomach is tight, like an iron cable is wrapped around my gut.

I sit down and stare at the table. Then I lift my head and watch as Grandpa picks up and plops the brown paper bag containing our Chinese food onto the kitchen table. He unpacks it. As if nothing happened. But I can see his face is gray.

Amazingly, our Chinese food is hot and in perfect condition, except for one flattened wonton. I don't know what's more surprising: that or a three-headed dog.

Neither one of us says a word. I know I have no idea *what* to say. I watch Grandpa walk over to the cabinet next to the fridge. He takes out a bottle of single-malt scotch. The expensive stuff.

To be clear, my grandpa drinks only three times a year. He has a stiff scotch to toast the New Year. He has a stiff scotch on the anniversary of my grandmother's death. And he toasts her silently on their wedding anniversary date. He opens another cabinet and pulls out a large tumbler. His hands shake as he pours himself the biggest, stiffest scotch I have ever seen him drink. He finishes half of it with one swig. Then he adds some ice cubes and comes and sits at the table.

"Well, that was a weird one," he whispers.

"Um, understatement of the year."

I wait. I wait for him to tell me more, but he doesn't. So I start, "Grandpa . . . I have the feeling there's a lot you're not telling me. Stuff you know. Stuff you've always known, maybe. About Mom. Me. Why she has her disease." I think back to his Internet history. Something isn't right. "And it's time to tell me."

He sips his scotch and starts to spoon his Chinese food onto his plate.

"Where do I even begin?"

"Why don't we try the beginning? Unless maybe you want to start with Cerberus and Evil Eyes. And how you don't seem too surprised that they showed up on our doorstep."

He sips his scotch again. He unwraps his chopsticks. Then he nods. "The beginning is with your mother, I suppose. When she was about your age."

He smiles at me. "You look like her, you know."

"Stop stalling." I give him a half smile.

He nods. "Well, she started having dreams. Vivid dreams. Dreams that were so real to her that your grandmother and I doubted her sanity. We loved her more than life itself, but our brilliant, charming, beautiful daughter would have a dream and then swear she saw something from her dream in real life."

I stop, a chopstick-skewered shrimp halfway to my lips. "And you didn't believe her?"

"We didn't know *what* to believe. She had never lied to us—unless you count the one time she tried drinking with her friend Shane. And after *that* hangover, she never tried it again. But I mean, it does sound a little crazy. Impossible."

"No crazier than a three-headed dog in our front yard."

He smiles a little. "No, I suppose not."

I eat a forkful of rice, not even positive I can keep it down after everything that's happened. I sip my Diet Coke. Then I hold my breath a little and wait for him to continue.

"We were worried. She didn't have many friends. You know how smart she is. She was very into her studies. Girl genius. Didn't quite fit in at school. Plus she was so beautiful, I think other girls were a little jealous of her. And she seemed more interested in her dream world than the real one. She sketched elaborate, beautiful—and sometimes scary—drawings of things she saw in her dreams. This was when she was thinking she might be a painter. So we took her to some fancy psychologist in Manhattan, with three degrees and an office on Park Avenue. He said it was something called lucid dreaming. Something about dreams being much more vivid and real than the way normal people dream."

I put my chopsticks down on my plate. "And then what?"

"Well, like most teenagers, she stopped confiding in her parents so much. She went off to Vassar and majored in art history. Graduated first in her class. We were so incredibly proud of her, Grandma and me. Then your mom went to graduate school—and of course excelled. Got a job at the museum. Worked her way up to a curator position. And got pregnant. With you. We were delighted we were going to be grandparents. We didn't ask a lot of questions. We didn't care that your father was a . . . um . . ."

"A sperm donor." Only I've always wondered about that story. Maybe now more than ever.

Grandpa stands. "Exactly. She had an important career, and the right man just never came along. Or so she told us. She just wanted to be a mother. It wasn't as if she needed a man for financial support. She was always so damn independent. A stubborn streak a mile wide. One minute." He goes down the hall to his room, and I hear him rummaging through a drawer or something. He comes back with a photograph. He doesn't hand it over to me right away but looks down at it.

"Your grandmother and I"—he points to his nose—"we could sniff out when something didn't quite add up. And so despite your mother's talk of a donor, we always assumed she would have at least discussed it with us first. So we had our doubts. And . . . we think this man is actually your father, not a donor."

I take the picture, my hands trembling so bad, I have to put the picture down on the table so I can look at it clearly. It is a picture of a dark-haired man with hair the same shade as mine—and curls, too—and my mom. I stare at him.

My entire life, I never had a father. But there he is. In the picture, my mother is pregnant. And smiling. Smiling in a way I don't think I've ever seen her smile. Pure happiness. They say pregnant women glow, and she is beaming. The two of them are not facing the camera. Like someone snapped the picture secretly. When they weren't looking.

"Who took this?"

"Your grandmother. We weren't spying. I promise you, Iris, we really weren't. But when she was pregnant with you, your mom said twice in one week she had a 'dinner engagement.' This was unusual. She never talked about dinners out or dating. Only work—exhibits and collections and donors. And at the end of her pregnancy, she was so tired, she would generally come home, call Grandma to check in—Grandma was her birthing coach—and read or rest. So we just *happened* to show up at your mom's favorite restaurant in Manhattan—Il Giardino—sort of hoping we might run into her. But then we saw her and suddenly thought better of being so nosy. We thought she might be mad. So Grandma just quietly snapped that picture."

The man in the photo looks familiar. Weirdly so. He also doesn't look real. I mean, he looks *human* enough, but he looks like a painting. From the Renaissance or something. Long black curly hair frames his face—I guess that's where I get my hair from. And his skin is so smooth and pale, it looks almost like marble.

A strange tingle makes me shiver. Then it hits me. "Wait, I know him," I whisper. "He's from a painting!"

My grandfather nods. "Sort of."

I leap from the table and go to the tall stack of my mom's coffee-table books in the living room. She has dozens of them—glossy, heavy books filled with pictures of art. They are still scattered across the floor after that scene with our strange visitor. I furiously leaf through one, then another, then another until I find it.

A painting. From 1811. By Pierre-Narcisse Guérin. Of the god Morpheus. The god of dreams.

He's with the goddess Iris. I am named for her. She is a messenger. She links the gods and humanity.

I run back to Grandpa and toss the book on the table. "Here!" I put my finger on the slick page. "He looks *exactly* like this painting! Exactly!"

Grandpa looks up at me. "I know."

"The Underworld—that guy who was just here threatening me told me to stay out of the Underworld."

Grandpa nods. "I had no idea you were in real danger, Iris. I would have told you all this sooner. But I just didn't know where to start. I've pressed your mother to talk to you, but she was afraid it would be too much for you to understand just yet. I think she wanted you to get through high school first. She will be so upset that you were actually hurt." He reaches out his hand to my cheek, where I am sure I am developing a nice, ugly bruise. "And then of course, her illness . . . she didn't want to add to your stress. You already have enough to deal with for a girl your age."

I start pacing. "Now I really have gone crazy. This can't be. This can't be, Grandpa." No wonder he didn't react with shock when Evil Eyes showed up. "All right . . . being as it's spill-family-secrets time, I'm going to tell you something. *Show* you something."

I lift up my leg and stick it on the table with a thud that rattles the plates, and then I pull up my jeans. I show him my ankle. The sharp scarlet of the vine imprint is still there, along with pinpricks of red. "This is *my* secret. I dreamed I was being pulled by vines. In a place. The place with the doors. The place I always dream about. And when I woke up, it was like it really happened. And I had these marks. And there was blood on my sheets. And then when I was hypnotized, I had a sort of dream, I guess. With these guys in dark suits and mirrored sunglasses. And afterward, I saw those same guys from my dream when Annie and I were driving down the street. In real life. And she saw them, too, so I'm not making it up. I didn't imagine it. She saw them. They were here. Just like the three-headed dog. Just like the man with the eyes. So . . . am I crazy?"

45

"Not crazy, exactly."

"The Underworld. Morpheus. That painting. Is my father really a god, one from the Underworld?"

My grandfather nods solemnly. "You've heard of dysfunctional families, right?"

"Yeah."

"Well, Lambie, you're from the most dysfunctional family in the world. Or rather the Underworld."

"You're saying . . ." I am starting to hyperventilate.

"The gods. You're part of them. On your father's side. Your father is the god of dreams. And the fact that he has a human daughter—or half-human daughter, I guess—isn't exactly making the rest of the Underworld happy. Put it this way . . . I wouldn't expect we'll invite them for Christmas."

I take my leg down from the table and plop into my chair.

I'd tell Grandpa he was nuts. Except he's really a very sensible man.

But more than that. Now that he's said it—out loud—some things I've always wondered about almost make sense.

A single dream is more powerful than a thousand realities.
NATHANIEL HAWTHORNE

Later that night, I keep staring at the photo and the painting. And I replay a memory from when I was little again and again, like finding a seashell and turning it over in my hand different ways, studying it. The problem is, I don't know whether it was a dream or real, and no matter how much I study it, it feels like grasping at fog. And now, of course, after all that's happened in the past few hours, my dreams and my reality are all a jumble. As if the real world and the dream world exist together all the time somehow.

My mom took me to the museum where she curated an exhibit of Greek sculpture. Maybe I was six. The tail end of kindergarten. We were there late. A security guard in a gray uniform came and told her he was going to be locking the building and she needed to finish up. She would be just a minute, she told him, just checking one last item. The guard left. And then a man emerged from behind a tall marble column. The man from the photo—the man from the painting. And he knelt down in the hush of the great hall and hugged me, and he told my mother I was beautiful. He whispered "Iris" in my ear. "Iris . . . what a beautiful name you have."

And then he was gone. My mom was crying. I asked her why. And she said she was both happy and sad. That I would understand when I was a grown-up. Only, here I am, pretty grown up, and none of it makes sense.

There is something else strange in this day of strangeness. The photo is seventeen years old. And it's faded a bit. The colors not as vibrant as I am sure they were when it was printed. Except for him— Morpheus. In the photo his colors are *more* vivid. It's as if the photo is in sepia tones, and he alone has been rendered in Photoshop, using colors richer than real life.

I want to think none of this is true, that I am in fact dreaming. But there's the little matter of the broken Don Mattingly bat. Of Grandpa confirming what I saw. I *saw* the man with the evil eyes. I *felt* his fingers digging into my face. He was as real as I am. I have the bruise to prove it.

I look at my alarm clock. Midnight. When I fall asleep, is the place I go to the Underworld? Is that why Evil Eyes warned me to stay away? Maybe it's not the insomnia at all that makes me different. Maybe it's where I go when I shut my eyes. And if I go there, will the man with the evil eyes, or the other men in suits, or the strange gods and beasts of the Underworld be there? Will they kill me for real? My face throbs from where Evil Eyes grabbed me.

I need to know more about Morpheus. My *father*. Even thinking that word feels strange to me. And thinking I have a father and not a donor is one thing. Being part goddess—forget that—even *thinking* I might be part of that world, part god, is too insane even to contemplate. Again, my head feels as if it's going to burst. My temples throb. My eyes burn.

I pull out my iPhone, hold my arm out, and take a selfie. I tap on the photo I've just taken, zoom in. The bruise is ugly. It is real. It is on my face. It is in the shape of finger marks, four stripes on one cheek leading down to my jawline. A thumb mark on the other side.

I keep staring at the photo on my phone, waiting to accept, somehow, what it means.

Gods are real.

I look over at the photo of my father that I have now tacked to my bulletin board. The photo of my father tells me I am part of them somehow.

And the destruction of our living room tells me that gods—and creatures—from the Underworld are after me. For something I can't control. My dreams.

This is my new reality.

And I want to wake from it. Only this is my waking life.

I need my mother to come out of her latest sleep state. I desperately need to talk to her.

But for now, I start on my computer. I told Grandpa earlier that I saw his browser history, that I know he hasn't been researching Sleeping Beauty syndrome. Grandpa 'fessed up that he's been studying Greek mythology. He sent me a bunch of links. A crash course on my relatives.

Shaking. I click on the first link.

Turns out, I have a very weird family tree.

Morpheus is one of the Oneiroi—gods of dreams, nightmares, death, and darkness. Morpheus is the son of Nyx, the goddess of night, which I guess makes her my grandmother. Only I don't see her baking chocolate chip cookies and coming to my high school graduation next year. I certainly don't expect her to give me a car.

And my father has brothers. One of his brothers is Hypnos, or Sleep. One brother controls nightmares. They are all related to Death. And apparently, according to Grandpa's theories, these uncles of mine are furious I exist. Sure, apparently thousands of years ago, the gods liked to meddle in human affairs. They even *had* affairs and so there were half-human, half-god children running around. But not anymore. For some reason, the gods decided to keep to themselves and stay hidden from mortals. So the idea of Morpheus falling in love with my mom? Real love. Grandpa thinks that made the Underworld really, really angry. And then having a real, live daughter in *this* century? Grandpa's right. We're not all spending Christmas together.

But what about Sebastian? He's in my dreams—he's the man *of* my dreams. How does he fit into this world? Is he a god?

And *then* I wonder exactly how I'm going to tell Annie all this. How I could tell anyone this:

"Oh, by the way . . . I have a confession to make. *I'm a freak*—half god half mortal." Like what does that even *mean*? Even Annie would think I'm nuts.

I'd be better off having the stigmata.

I read more, Googling like crazy. It's overwhelming and exhausting. My eyelids are heavy. I look at the time function on my computer. It's 2:22 in the morning. I put my head down on my desk. Resting for just a second.

I am in the long hallway of many doors, and the keys I carry jangle at my side. I hear a voice. His voice. But I don't see him. The voice is in my head. And his voice says, "Come to our secret hiding place. Remember, Iris? Remember?"

But I don't remember. At least I don't think so. I look down at my key ring, and I see a key. A tiny key. It's one of hundreds, but I can tell it's special. And it looks so familiar. At the top of it a leaf is engraved, so small and yet so detailed. I touch the key, and it's warm. So now I have the key, but how am I to tell which door it opens? I walk down the hallway. Behind me I hear growls like thunder in the distance. I don't want to look back. I refuse to. I want to find the door that belongs to this key. I'm frightened. The hallway is dark. So dark. And I am so, so utterly and completely afraid.

I see a door. A small one, no taller than three feet high. A small door for a small key. That sort of

*makes sense. The door has a carving of a tree on it.
I lean down and insert the key. I turn it to the right.
Click.*

*I get down on my hands and knees and open
the door. Squirming just so, I crawl through, not
knowing for sure what is on the other side.*

*But as soon as my head is through, I see it's a
beautiful garden, and in the middle of the garden is
a tall, magnificent tree.*

*I finish squeezing through the door, shut it behind
me, and stand up on the other side. It's peaceful.
Birds are chirping, and I can hear in the distance
the gentle sound of the sea. I follow a soft, sandy
path through phlox and lavender and hollyhocks.
Their scents mix with the smell of the ocean, and I
make my way to the tree. It's an old oak, with a thick
trunk and branches that reach skyward but seem to
stretch out so far I can barely see their ends. As I
walk closer, I realize it's my oak tree. Mine. The tree
from my front yard. And in it is my tree house, the
tree house I have played in since kindergarten.*

*I smile and touch the trunk of the tree. It feels real
beneath my fingers. I start to climb up the wooden
boards Grandpa nailed into the trunk. But as I look
at them, I realize they're new, just like when he first
built my special fortress in the branches the summer
before I started school—not worn and weathered*

like in the real world. But it's definitely my tree house. My secret hiding place. I smile, and I feel as if I'm five again.

I pass through the small trapdoor that leads into the tree house, and I see a little boy inside. He looks familiar.

He grins at me. His hair is long and black and wavy. He has two dimples. He's playing with marbles, but he stops and says, "I've been waiting for you, Iris."

I look down at my hands. I am five. I am a little girl. I sit down cross-legged next to him and put my elbows on my knees and smile back at him.

"Hi." I want to say his name. I am certain it is Sebastian, though I have never seen this boy before. But I am afraid to say the name out loud. I think maybe then the gods will come. The gods who want to hurt me.

"Want to play checkers? Or pirates? Or . . . want to look through the telescope?"

"The telescope," I say eagerly.

We stand and arrange the tripod of the telescope so it faces out the window. I peer through, and I can see far, far away, to a sea. A beautiful sea, shining and serene, gentle cresting waves dancing on its surface. I see a pirate ship in the distance, its skull-and-crossbones flag snapping in the wind.

He slips his hand in mine, and I look over at him.

"I'm going to marry you someday, Iris." He reaches out the window and points to a branch and brushes the leaves aside. "Look." And there he has carved a heart. And inside the heart is S + I.

We hear a noise, the growling of a dog. We exchange worried looks and both scoot down and move to the corner of the tree house to hide. We huddle together, and the growling grows louder. My heart thuds so loudly, it sounds as if it's in my head.

"They'll find us," I whisper.

"No, they won't." He puts his index finger to his lips. Our faces are inches from each other. I think he's going to kiss me. And that somehow this kiss will change my life. But then we hear the growls turn into full-fledged barking. Many dogs. Vicious ones, by the sounds of them.

Suddenly, Sebastian isn't five. He's older. Seventeen maybe, eighteen? And so am I. He is still holding my hand, and now I don't know whether my heart is pounding because we're touching or because of the beasts below the tree house. I look into his eyes—they are almost black, they are so dark—and I realize I have known him my whole life.

"Go!" he urges.

"No!"

He shakes his head. "I will find you. Just go." He points to the tree-house window, then stands and *half lifts, half pushes me out. I am on a thick tree branch, sliding my way along its rough bark. Down below, I see Cerberus. I hear angry voices. Someone shouts, "There she is!"*

I panic. And then I lose my balance.

I scream and fall to earth.

And I am awake. I gasp. Like I really fell. I look at the clock. It's only 2:26. It was a dream. It wasn't reality, since I'm sitting inside my house. Or was I transported to the Underworld? How could I have traveled to the Underworld and back in just four minutes? Where is the Underworld? Is it a place, like when people believe they go to Heaven when they die?

I shut down my computer, then quietly leave my room and creep through the house to the living room. Grandpa and I have cleaned up the mess and the broken lamp, but I still feel the something terrible that happened in this long, strange night.

I peer out the front door at my tree house. That meeting with young Sebastian—did that really happen? I know what I have to do. I grab a flashlight from the desk drawer and then open the front door and listen. I don't hear anything. Not a dog growling, nothing. Just wind rustling the leaves, and far-off traffic. I slip out the door and run, barefoot, to the tree house.

I've been up and down this tree so many times in my life, I can practically do it blindfolded. I slide into the house, dusty and dirty with neglect; there are old autumn leaves on the floor. I smile. I can't remember how many nights Annie and I slept up here.

I turn on the flashlight and go to the window. I point the flashlight, but I don't see anything on the tree. No carving. Nothing.

My heart falls flat. Maybe I'm insane, after all, thinking the dream world and this world somehow mingle together—at least where I am concerned. But part of me is certain it will be here, somewhere.

So I lean out the window farther, sliding a knee up so I'm halfway out of the tree house. I move branches and leaves. I focus the beam of light against the trunk.

And I find it.

A heart carved into the trunk.

S + I.

And carved next to it:

4 EVER.

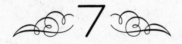

7

All that we see or seem
Is but a dream within a dream.
EDGAR ALLAN POE

Annie and I have been best friends since the first day of second grade when she moved in two blocks away. We used to in-line skate down the street together. We even had strep together. In fact, I spent the entire week I had strep at the Caseys' house so I wouldn't give it to Grandpa. Though then there were only three Casey kids, and we all had strep at the same time. Annie is the person I told about my first real kiss (Mike Shanahan, summer before seventh grade). She's the person I cried to when my mom first got sick.

But how do you tell someone the truth about yourself if that truth sounds like a big, fat, made-up lie?

But she believes me.

"You do?" I ask.

"Obviously. I mean, *come on*!"

"Um, no offense, Annie, it happened to me, and *I* don't even really believe it. Not a hundred percent."

Both of us are flopped on my bed eating popcorn. Some stupid reality show is on, and I think if they filmed *my* life, no one would believe it. But it might get good ratings. Drama. Romance. Danger.

"First of all, I know your grandfather. Have known him as long as I've known you. I know he loves two things in this world more than anything. The Yanks. And you. And only if some crazy guy with a three-headed dog was trying to rip your face off would he use *that* bat as a weapon—and break it! His Mattingly bat! So it has to be true."

I smile at her logic. That's my Annie.

"*And* don't forget. I saw those *Men in Black* guys. And your ankle. And now the bruise on your face. Do you know it's a combination of green, yellow, purple, and red?"

"Don't remind me. I look hideous."

"All right then, so your dad is not a sperm donor. He's a god. So, like, what does that really mean? Do you have special powers or something?"

I shrug. "I wish I knew."

"And will this mean he starts coming to parent-teacher conferences? 'Hi, this is my dad. He's a god.' And what about the guy—the man of your dreams?"

"Annie, I don't know. I've never, ever, ever felt like that around someone. Not even when I went to prom with Charlie."

Charlie Jacobs was my *major* sophomore-year crush. He was a senior, and now he's off at Brown. We e-mail each other still, and I saw him over his fall break. And I thought he was gorgeous—still think he's gorgeous—but it's different. When I see Sebastian, when I hear his voice, my insides do somersaults. And backflips. That's about as best as I can explain it.

"I wish you could ask someone about all this," Annie says.

"Me, too."

We hear a knock on my door. "Yeah?" I say, assuming that it's Grandpa.

But when the door opens, it's my mother.

I scream "*Mom!*" and jump up from bed to hug her. "God, you have no idea how much I need to talk to you."

She smiles weakly. "I think I do. I hear life has been pretty exciting while I've been sleeping."

"How'd you hear that?"

"Grandpa. I woke up, and he filled me in. Then he sent me in here." She furrows her brow at the sight of my bruise and reaches out to touch it.

I wince. "It looks worse than it is. But I could use a little less excitement. And I have a *lot* of questions."

"I'm sure. I presume you've told Annie . . ." Her voice trails off.

"Everything."

She smiles. "I figured. All right, you two, come with me to the kitchen. I need to eat. Carbs! Come on, and I'll tell you all that I know. The story I should have told you sooner. The story I wish I'd had the nerve to tell you."

Annie and I follow Mom. I don't know how long we have until she falls back to sleep—we never know. So I need to be sure I ask her everything.

∽

My mom carb-loads like a linebacker.

We watch her eat a huge plate of spaghetti covered in Ragú. Yeah. She's not winning any cooking awards. In between forkfuls, she tells me about my father.

"First, my darling, I am so sorry. More than you could possibly know. I knew *eventually* I would have to tell you the truth. But I didn't want to burden you. It's too much. Too impossible. I should have told you sooner, but I kept waiting until I thought you could handle it."

"I understand." I mean, when is the right time to tell your kid she's part goddess?

"Where to start...? At some point," Mom continues, "the gods decided to keep out of human affairs. Mostly. They are a tricky bunch, though. They break promises. Lie. Cheat. Kill. Have crazy love affairs. Sort of like a giant Underworld soap opera."

I was right. I could be a reality show.

"But for centuries and centuries, all the way until now, most of the gods have wanted to be unseen by humans, to keep out of our world—most of the time anyway. But the dream world has always been something else. Someplace neither here nor there."

"I dream of the hallway of many doors. It *feels* so real. And I know my body is in my bed. But I feel like I travel someplace. A different world that's not reality but is more than a dream."

She nods.

"I have dreams about forgetting my homework," Annie moans. "Nothing exciting."

"Look at my face," I say to Annie. "You don't want exciting, I promise you."

Annie winces. "Sorry. I guess I didn't mean it quite that way."

My mother sips her ice water. Then she continues. "Iris and I are rare. We dream in a different way. It really is this other world. This other way we dream. In her case, it's because of who her father is. In my case, I'm a lucid dreamer."

"I still don't get what that is," Annie says.

"I assume somewhere back in time, centuries ago, when the gods were meddling in human affairs, lucid dreamers were touched by the gods. Edgar Allan Poe said all that we see or seem is but a dream within a dream. Some of his imagery . . . I think he went to the Underworld. In fact, I think some of the most creative people—writers and painters—they have glimpses of that faraway place."

Annie looks at my mom. "I can believe some painters go there—like that guy who painted the melted clocks."

Mom laughs. "Dalí? Yeah, I can believe that. But for most it's just a glimpse, this little flicker of a glimpse, those occasional dreams that you *swear* are real. Feelings of déjà vu. Ever have a dream you just don't want to wake up from? Or worse, a nightmare so real you're desperate to wake up because it's just too vivid, too real? And all your senses seem to be telling you that it's real. That's the glimpses most people get. But for me, for Iris, *all* our dreams are like that."

"When I dream, I swear it's real. Like last night I dreamed of a tree, and I touched the bark. And I could smell the salt in the air from the sea in the distance. I heard the wind rustle the leaves." I leave out touching Sebastian. Holding his hand.

My mother adds, "It's like everyone else dreams in black and white, or maybe color, but she and I dream in high def. We *go* there. Actually, literally, go there. And one night, when I was a little older than Iris, I had a dream, and I saw him."

"Morpheus?" Annie asks, hanging on my mom's every word.

Mom nods. "You know that scene in the *The Wizard of Oz* where Toto pulls the curtain back?"

"Yeah," I say. Mom knows it's my favorite old movie. Every year, Grandpa and I buy gobs of junk food and watch it. And I still freak out over the flying monkeys. They get me every time.

"Well, just like in that scene, Morpheus was the Wizard. I don't know, but I remember having this dream, and suddenly, I was thinking—in my dream— that I could see the man on the edges of the dream, controlling my dream. I was aware I was dreaming— *that* is lucid dreaming. I could *see* him. Only that was supposed to be impossible. He was supposed to be behind the curtain. I turned to him—in my dream—and spoke to him. How? How could I see him? Then he told me it was because he had fallen in love with me. That he was drawn to me."

"So what happened?" I ask. Not the typical how-your-parents-got-together story.

She smiles. "Like anyone with a crush, I started *trying* to find him. And soon, it got easier and easier. Every night, in my dreams, we would meet. I never wanted to leave. I was . . . in love. But sooner or later, I realized I needed to belong to this world. Have a life in this world. But how do you break up with a god?" She blushes. "But he loves me. He followed me here. He's a god. He can take human form if he wishes."

My eyes widen. "And?"

"And . . . there you are, my beautiful daughter." She smiles. "One night of passion. I am a lesson for high school girls everywhere. It takes only one time to get pregnant if you aren't careful." She points a finger. "So pay attention to that lesson, you two."

"So first you tell me my father is a Greek god. Now you tell me I'm an accident. Wonderful."

"Oh, Iris . . . no. We were thrilled. Thrilled and sad. Sad because, I mean, I think we realized we couldn't live this sort of white-picket-fence existence. That it would be *complicated*. But to have a child with the man . . . the god . . . that I loved? When I was with him, I could barely breathe. It is still as thrilling as when I first saw him. I love him, Iris. I still do and always will."

"Do you still go there to be with him? Is that why you sleep? Is that what your disease is?" I feel kind of hurt that she would choose going there instead of being here, with me.

"No. You are my reason for living, Iris. It's a lot more complicated than that."

"*Complicated.* Why does everyone keep using that word? I am so going to have Daddy issues after this. I mean, hasn't he ever wanted to be part of my life?"

"He's tried to be so careful, Iris. To protect you. But he's been there. Sometimes. When he can."

"Come on, Mom. I have one weird memory—I think—of meeting him at the museum. Did he step out of a painting? But that's it. He's not part of my life." Maybe it was better when I thought he was an anonymous donor. My mother told me she'd selected him because his profile said he was a member of Mensa. Who spoke four languages. And volunteered for Greenpeace. All a lie. He was actually a *god*. "He's never tried to be there for me."

"He has. That was him. At the museum. And Santa Claus."

"If you tell me Santa Claus is real, Mom, I swear—"

"No, Iris. Remember when I took you to meet Santa Claus at the mall? You were seven and just on the cusp of not believing—thanks to Joey D. from your bus stop—who told *everyone* that Santa was a fake. Anyway, we went to Macy's, and the regular Santa was on break and you went and sat on the substitute Santa's lap. Remember? He was so fascinated by you? He talked to you for twenty minutes, asking you all sorts of questions about your grades and your interests. The other kids and parents in line started getting angry."

I scrunch my face, struggling to remember.

"And your fourth-grade piano recital. Think about the janitor offstage. Remember how he applauded for you louder than anyone in the audience? And he gave you a hug after. Think about his eyes."

As soon as she says this, I feel as if a spider is crawling up my spine. The eyes. The gentleness. The color—a stormy gray not like any other eyes I have ever seen. The eyes of the janitor. Of the Santa. Of the man at the museum.

I look over at Annie. I feel tears pushing at me, tears

I don't want to shed. Not yet. I need to understand more. Annie smiles at me, encouraging me. "See? Your dad loves you."

Annie's dad tries to arrange his schedule so he can go to all her soccer games. Those are the times I miss having a father of my own. I swallow. "My dad has shown up in my life?"

Mom nods. "Not in the way he wants to, Iris. But in the safest way he can, to draw no attention to you. He loves you so dearly. And so the reason I sleep so much . . ." She pauses and takes a deep breath. "Iris, I leave you to go to the Underworld to protect you. Your father is warring with his brothers. And I am by his side.

"Among the Oneiroi, there has never been a half-human child born. And his brothers—Thanatos, death, and Epiales, nightmares—they're jealous and angry. They think your father made a careless and foolish mistake."

My mother looks at me hard and grabs my hand. "Iris, you've been going to the Underworld in your dreams. And I know you—I know you didn't even realize that's where you've been going, not until now. I know that you can't help going there, that you aren't controlling it. But it's dangerous for you. The brothers—your uncles—think you will usher in a new age of communication between the Underworld and the human world. And they're against it. Violently so. And they will stop at nothing to make sure you keep to your own world."

I stare at her. I can hardly believe what she's saying, but somehow it all makes sense.

"One of them was already here. I don't know which one, though—the one with the strange eyes."

"Epiales. The god of nightmares, the things you don't want to think about."

"And what about . . ." I hold my breath a minute. "What about Sebastian?"

Mom smiles. "I've met him. He's your dream guardian."

"My what?"

"Born when you were. A product of your father's world. A way to protect you from your nightmares. To keep you safe."

I think of the times in the hallway of many doors when I chose the wrong door. When I was lost in darkness, chased by monsters and alligators, trapped in small places and unable to breathe. And I remember the voice that comforted me. Always. Calling to me. Telling me the way out.

"I don't know why your connection is so fierce, so

strong. I suppose it's a bit like your father and me. But he's of that world, Iris. He's an immortal." Her face grows cloudy. "I can tell you that if you two are determined to be together somehow, it can only mean trouble and a great deal of heartache. I know the pull of that world. Of the gods. I know it all too well. I wish you two weren't drawn to each other. I want you to have a normal life."

"Um, Mom . . . maybe you should have thought of that *before* you conceived me with the god of dreams."

Annie shakes her head. "This is some of the weirdest but coolest stuff I've ever heard in my life. To think, my best friend is half goddess."

Mom eats spaghetti, and I try to absorb what she's told me. Then Mom stands up and says, "I'll be right back."

She walks to her room and returns a few minutes later. She's holding a business card. She stares down at it and crinkles her nose, as if she's trying to decide what to do.

"I was hoping, I really was, that you weren't like me. It's part of why I never told you all this. Part of why I hid it from Grandma and Grandpa. You know, Grandpa's guessed some of the connection, but I've never really talked about it. Not completely. But you've always known you were different. Haven't you?"

I nod. My dreams have always felt so real. I remember sitting in the cafeteria while this girl on Annie's soccer team was blathering on about a dream, and it sounded so . . . boring, flat, even. Not like mine. And now? I think of my ankle. Of the tree trunk. I'm not sure where my dream world ends and the real one begins—or even if there's a difference for me.

"I was hoping you *could* be normal. Like every other little girl in the world . . . normal. But when you started with your insomnia, I had a feeling you were different. Then, though he hated to upset me, about six months ago your father said you'd been spotted in the Underworld. The Keres chased you out."

I shiver. "The Keres?"

"Your aunts. Death spirits. Mist. They hunger for human blood and still hover over this world sometimes, searching for dying souls. They are vicious—and very jealous."

"Jealous? Of what?"

"You are of both worlds. And you don't realize that you are so, so lovely, while they . . . thirst for death? I don't know, Iris. I can only guess."

"What can I do? I don't know how *not* to go there.

I just . . . go. I don't know what to do." And though I don't say it out loud, part of me doesn't care if it's dangerous. I need to see Sebastian again. My head hurts from all of this.

Mom hands me the business card. "You can go see one of your relatives."

"But you just said my relatives want to kill me."

"A *different* relative. She left the Underworld. She came to live among humans."

I look down at the fancy vellum card. It smells faintly of exotic perfume.

APHRODITE MATCHMAKING SERVICE
FIND YOUR TRUE LOVE MATCH
APHRODITE CYPRIS, MATCHMAKER TO THE STARS

I look at Mom.

She shakes her head. "Your father and I are doing everything we can to protect you in the Underworld. But the men with mirrored glasses, Epiales, Cerebus . . . Iris, they're coming here. That man who attacked you and Grandpa is the god of nightmares. And I promise you, Iris"—she shivers slightly—"what he did here is just a hint of what he's capable of. But go see Aphrodite. She's also from the Underworld. She can guide you, Iris. Even better than I can. She can help you. Go see her, please."

I look down at the business card.

I may have been scared by the man with the evil eyes, but I know that I need to find out more about my father. About who I really am. About Sebastian.

I look at Annie. "You're coming with me, right?"

She grins. "Like you could keep me away. I mean, I thought it was cool when you maybe had stigmata. This is *way* better."

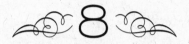

*Much of our waking experience
is but a dream in the daylight.*
GEORGE ELIOT

By midnight, Mom has fallen back in her Sleeping Beauty state. Annie stays over. Only she actually sleeps, despite three Red Bulls. I toss and turn, and sleep comes in snatches—and I don't dream, which is almost a relief.

The next day dawns with flurries. Annie and I take the bus into Manhattan, all decked out like a glittering Christmas present, windows wrapped in green and red and tinsel and expensive displays of visions of Christmases past, present, and future, and extravagances Annie and I can only wish for. On street corners Salvation Army Santas ring their bells. Annie and I huddle close to each other as we face into the wind. Then we descend into the warmth beneath the ground and get on the subway. We make our way all the way out to Queens on the N line, which should take us to the address for Aphrodite Cypris. When we climb the subway steps back up into the cold, I laugh.

"What?"

"Is there any doubt which building is hers?"

I point. A Greek restaurant named Mount Olympus stands in the middle of the block. As we draw closer, I see statues of the Greek gods and colonnades. When we cross the street, I hear Greek music blasting out.

According to the voice-mail message when I tried calling this morning, Aphrodite is on the second floor. The smells from the restaurant are heavenly and make my stomach growl. I now have a craving for a gyro or baklava. Annie and I try the door, but it's locked. I press the button next to mailbox slots. A voice calls out from the intercom.

"Who *is* it?" It is a woman's voice, singsongy and high-pitched.

And suddenly, it's as if my mouth doesn't work. On the train out to Queens, I had practiced in my head what I was going to say. But now the words are stuck. Exactly who is it ringing the bell? Me, Iris . . . half human, half . . . and I can't even finish the idea. In fact, the idea, in the light of day, makes me kind of nauseous. She cannot really be *the* Aphrodite any more than I can be the daughter of Morpheus.

"Who is it?" the voice on the intercom asks more insistently.

Annie leans close to the speaker. "It's Morpheus's daughter. Her name is Iris."

I elbow Annie and stare at her. On the train, as I had rehearsed things, I certainly wasn't going to blurt *that* out first thing. It seems like the kind of thing you have to warm up to saying out loud.

The intercom is silent for several long moments. We press the button to her apartment again, while the loud Greek music continues to play. My heart sort of sinks in my chest. If Aphrodite won't see us, then I have no idea where to turn. Except maybe the hypnotherapist. But Aphrodite's the one I really need. Then we hear a loud buzzing sound, and a click. We try the door, and it opens. Annie and I step inside. I take off my gloves and shove them into my purse. I rub my hands together and blow on them.

"Man," Annie whispers. "This is *so* tacky." She unbuttons her coat.

Painted all the way up the hallway is an immense mural. Gods and goddesses frolic on fluffy white clouds.

"Here goes nothing," I say, and start climbing the stairs, Annie right behind me. When we get to the second-story landing, there's only one apartment on the floor. I press the buzzer next to the door. After a moment, the door swings open, and I am face to face with Aphrodite, the goddess of love.

Only she isn't what I expect at all. Aphrodite is supposed to be beautiful—this incredible womanly goddess no man can resist. And she *is* beautiful. But she's also . . . well, a big woman. My grandpa would say voluptuous (just his type!). She's definitely *very* plus size. Her hair is long and brown and lusciously curly. Her face is stunning, with perfect makeup. And she's blinged out to the max—rhinestone rings and stacks of clinking bracelets and big swingy earrings that shine. She's dressed in an evening gown—even though it's ten-thirty in the morning. The gown hugs her curves perfectly. But to be honest, she looks a little crazy.

"Iris!" she shrieks, and grabs me in a boob-smashing hug. "I wasn't expecting you just yet. Must mean trouble with the uncles."

"Hi . . . um . . . Ms. Cypris," I say when she finally releases me.

She slaps my arm playfully. "Get *out* of here. Call me *Aunt* Aphrodite! Come in, come in."

She half drags me by the hand. I gesture toward Annie. "This is—"

"Annie . . ." Aphrodite says. "I know."

Annie and I exchange glances. And then I get my first glimpse of the inside of Aphrodite's apartment.

If Annie called the mural tacky, I have no idea what she would call the apartment. It is crammed—and I mean crammed—with tchotchkes. The coffee table alone has at least fifteen snow globes. I squint. They are of the Parthenon and Greek tourist attractions.

Bookshelves are filled with books on Greece, but also little statues of Greek gods and goddesses. On the walls are Greek icons in gold inlay and rich and vibrant colors that conflict with one another, dozens of icons crowding for space. I almost don't know where to look—it's dizzying.

Aphrodite sees Annie and me looking around at all her cluttered possessions.

"I miss Greece. What can I say? I adore my things!" She picks up a snow globe that says I LOVE ATHENS inside and shakes it. She laughs loudly—a deep, rich belly laugh that makes me almost want to laugh, too. "Snow globes! They never get old! I also love dribble glasses. And magnets."

I glance into her kitchen. There is not a square inch on her refrigerator not covered with magnets.

She sweeps her hand toward the dining room table.

In the center is a silver candelabra made of cherubs, each holding a tapered, orchid-colored candle up in its arms. Now that I look around, there's a *lot* of pink and red in the apartment, from curtains to pillows. It is hideous.

"Come and sit. We have a lot to talk about, my darlings!"

Annie and I take off our coats and hang them on the backs of our chairs and then sit, and Aphrodite dances—literally—into the kitchen. She returns with plates laden with baklava and other pastries and three Cokes.

"I don't do Diet Coke," she says.

She plops into a chair and pops a pastry into her mouth.

I smile at her, feeling awkward. "So . . . ? You're Aphrodite."

She laughs again. I love her laugh. "I bet you were expecting a supermodel!" She eats another pastry and then looks at Annie. "Eat, you skinny thing. Pastries are good for the soul."

Annie takes a bite and looks at me, green eyes wide. "Oh my *God*, but these are awesome. They have to be, like . . . I don't know. Made by gods."

Aphrodite laughs again and bangs the table with

her hand. "Ha! No . . . these are made by Nico, down at the bakery on the corner. The guy is a god. You should see his body. But he's mortal. And can he bake! What a catch!"

I pick up a pastry, a tiny Greek wedding cookie. It melts in my mouth.

Aphrodite looks at me. "You should eat to enjoy. That's one reason I'm not a supermodel. And I'll tell you why . . . I am the goddess of *beauty*, and there is *nothing* more unattractive than a woman who believes her beauty is only in her body. A woman who can't eat a pastry and enjoy it. A woman who eats a pastry and mentally calculates how many miles she has to run on the treadmill to 'earn' that pastry. A woman who won't belly laugh. No. I am a goddess. I have thousands of years of experience in what makes beauty. And I can tell you, American women have it wrong. At the first sign of wrinkles, women Botox their faces. Have you ever seen anything so ridiculous?" She pulls back on her face and purses her lips to look like a plastic-surgery victim.

Annie smirks. "The lady next door to me has had her lips so plumped she looks like a duck. Ruined her face."

"Precisely!" Aphrodite says, releasing her face.

"Beauty, my darlings, is from within. It is from knowing *precisely* who you are and *loving* that person. And let me let you in on a little secret."

We lean closer toward her.

"I have to *fight* the men off," she whispers.

I look at Annie and grin. I love Aphrodite already.

"Now"—she spreads her hands palm down on the table—"I suppose you've come here because you have a lot of questions."

"Understatement," I say. Though I'm beginning to feel at home, I'm still a little nervous about starting down this rabbit hole of my family history. I glance at Annie.

Annie says, "I'll start. Why did you leave the Underworld?"

Aphrodite rolls her eyes. "The drama. The backstabbing. I guess I was tired of it all. So I came to live among the mortals. Maybe I just wanted a change. Maybe I just wanted Nico's pastries." She grins devilishly. "And Nico."

"But it's not like humans don't backstab, too," I say, thinking of the meanest girl in our high school, a girl in my English class—Harper. She's treacherous, spreading rumors about Annie and, worst of all, doing it all with a smile, pretending she is some churchgoing Goody Two-shoes. Meanwhile, she tries her hardest to destroy anyone she doesn't like. And she's never happy. She's always got some new enemy she has to get even with. Annie is only one of many. This week's frenemy. It will be someone else next week. And the week after that.

"I know." Aphrodite smiles. "But you all live, what? Seventy years? Eighty? Maybe ninety, if you never eat pastries or drink good wine? In god terms, you're pikers. Some of your behaviors are strangely endearing because you're *such* babies. But the dramas down in the Underworld? Honey, I've been living them for *centuries*. Besides, I *know* love and beauty. I really thought I could help people. And I do. I know when two people are meant to be together. I'm the world's best matchmaker."

I want to ask about Sebastian, but before I can, Annie blurts out, "So do you know who I'm supposed to be with?"

Aphrodite tosses her long hair behind her shoulders and laughs—squeals actually. "If I told you, you wouldn't believe me."

Annie grabs Aphrodite's arm. "*Please?* Please tell me."

"All right. You, Annie, are going to get married

when you're twenty-six. And you're going to be so happy—a soul-mate match. Zeus help me, I love those."

"Who?" Annie asks. "Do I know him?"

I know Annie is hoping it's Ryan, the goalie on the guys' soccer team. She's been crushing on him since eighth grade.

"In fact, you do."

Annie smiles.

Then Aphrodite says, "It's Henry Wu."

My mouth drops open. "Henry-in-math-class Henry?"

Annie adds, "Henry-with-the-GPA-of-4.35, sure-to-be-valedictorian-and-going-to-Harvard Henry?"

"Beanpole Henry?" I add. Henry Wu is six feet three and, despite eating five hot dogs every day for lunch, can't seem to gain an ounce—hasn't since junior high. He's just gotten taller. Aphrodite may be a goddess, but now I think she's delusional.

Annie shakes her head. "He is most certainly *not* my soul mate."

"Ah, but you can't see what I see. Henry, dear Henry, will pack on forty pounds in college rowing crew for Harvard. Wait till you see his biceps. He will invent the next Facebook."

"The *next* Facebook?" I ask.

"He'll be worth billions. Zillions."

"Henry Wu?" I ask incredulously.

"Yes. Henry Wu. But see the inner, my darlings. Despite being worth zillions, it won't change him. He's deep-down good. The very best kind of good, right down to the core. He won't become a player. And then he'll donate to Annie's foundation, the girl he's carried a torch for since freshman year of high school. And the rest, my little lovebirds, is all a matter of the heart."

"My foundation?" Annie asks. "What foundation?"

"The one you're going to establish. Teaching soccer to inner-city kids. Henry is going to fund the entire thing in eight years. He'll purchase land for you upstate to build a summer camp. Trust me. Henry Wu is a dreamboat in disguise. You just need to look a little closer. Pay attention to what really counts."

Annie looks stunned. But I have more important matters to discuss than Henry Wu. "What about Sebastian?"

"Ah, yes." Aphrodite's face grows serious. "The path from Annie to Henry Wu, while unlikely, is a simple one compared to yours. Tell me about how you *feel* when you see him."

My face flushes. It's so stupid. He's a *dream*. But I tell her anyway. "I had never actually seen him until the last two dreams. I'd just heard him. I've been hearing him for as long as I can remember. This voice. He would call for me to find him. Or sometimes, when I was having a nightmare, he would whisper to me not to be scared. I would hear that voice, and I would feel safe somehow. And even though I never saw him, I just knew deep down that the voice I heard was somehow . . ." I trail off.

"Your destiny," Aphrodite finishes.

"Yeah. Crazy, huh?"

"Not at all."

"And then, just a few days ago, I saw him."

"He's beautiful."

I nod.

"He loves you, Iris. He's been hiding in your dreams for a long time. He knows you. Knows what you're afraid of . . . your nightmares. Knows your hopes and dreams. It's an intimate place, the world of dreams. Dreams are unique to each dreamer. Sure, some dreams are universal—ever have the one where your teeth fall out? Or the one where you're falling?"

Annie and I both nod.

"I hate the teeth one," Annie says.

"But," Aphrodite continues, "each dreamer's dreams have symbols and clues uniquely theirs."

When I think about it, Sebastian knowing my dreams feels very strange—I feel exposed, almost like I'm naked. He knows so much about me, yet I know nothing about him.

"So you are two young lovers who need to find a way to be together," Aphrodite says.

"I guess. I don't really know him, but I . . . I want to. He said he wanted to come with me. Back here. But I don't know how that's possible. I'm . . . you know . . . human. Um, half human. And he's . . . a dream. Immortal."

"The passage back is crossing the River of Sorrows. Epiales and his realm—it's a vast, almost endless room of nightmares. What are your nightmares, Iris? What are you afraid of?"

"That's easy," I say, holding up my hand and counting off my top-five things to fear. "One, clowns."

"Clowns?" Annie asks. "Really?"

I shrug. "They freak me out."

"White paint, red noses, balloon animals." Annie shakes her head. "Terrifying." She rolls her eyes. "All right, keep going."

"Cockroaches. Spiders. The dark—I sleep with a light on," I say. "And rats."

Aphrodite looks at me intently. "Iris, those aren't nightmares."

"They are. I mean, those are the things I'm afraid of."

"No. For the god of nightmares, they're nothing. Nightmares, the worst of nightmares, are things you cannot even imagine. And why can't you imagine them right now? Because your mind just doesn't go there. Those are the things Epiales will use against you. The unspoken fears. The things you won't even *breathe* because they're just too horrible."

"Like in horror movies?" I ask. "Serial killers and all that?"

Aphrodite shakes her head. "Boogeymen are terrifying. That's what a horror movie is, after all. Replacing that childhood fear of what's hiding underneath the bed or in the closet with some awful imagining of it. But really? It doesn't take much imagination to invent a slasher film. They're not terribly clever."

"I hate them," Annie says.

"Take a woman and destroy her in the most sadistic way possible. Invent new ways to do it. Saws and machetes and . . ." Aphrodite shudders. "That's *entertainment*? Why are we entertained by that? Why should we appeal to the basest and ugliest of human nature? They're scary, but they're born of humans. No, Epiales will search deeper, deep inside your dreams for what you love. And he'll then try to take that away." She lowers her voice to a whisper. "I don't even want to give voice to how. I don't want to plant any ideas in your head, nothing for you to take *to* the Underworld in your dreams. But in order for Sebastian to come here, the two of you would have to pass through that realm of darkness, of the things you can't speak of."

I think of my nightmares. The really horrible ones of being chased by something, or the ones about being locked in a tiny, dark room. With rats. I exhale to calm myself.

"But aren't the gods supposed to be above this?" Annie asks. "They're gods, after all, not mortals with weaknesses like ours."

"Epiales may be a god," Aphrodite says, "but he's a jealous, angry god. The worst kind!"

"What is he jealous of?" I ask. That word again. Jealous. Why would anyone be jealous of *me*?

"Your humanity. Think of it, darling. He's the god of nightmares, living since the dawn of time in the ugliest part of the Underworld, on the far shores of Oceanus, in a place near eternal Night. He haunts people, playing with them like a cat toying with a mouse. But you have power, too, Iris."

If I have power, I'm not sure what it is. I certainly don't feel as though I'm in control here.

"*Own* your power. You are half goddess. You're stronger than you realize. And you have humanity— humanity is powerful. You have love—your mother, your grandfather, Annie . . . you have things you're not afraid to fight for. Use that. And any time you are really afraid, remember, *It's only a dream*."

"I know, but lately, my dreams follow me here." I think back to the attack on Grandpa and me. My bruise certainly feels real enough.

"Yes, I'm not surprised. But the gods are less powerful here. When we take human form, we can bleed. Gods can't defy physics in the mortal realm. At least not totally. You can defeat him."

"But if you saw how strong Epiales is . . ."

Aphrodite pats my hand. "You're strong, too. Koios will help you."

"My hypnotherapist? How do you—"

She smiles and throws her head back and howls her fabulous, authentic laugh. "Oh, sweetheart, we gods and goddesses have many tricks up our sleeves. Koios is one of us. The god of the inquisitive mind. He will teach you how to control your dreams. How to find Sebastian. How to bring him here. Now have another pastry."

Aphrodite pushes the plate toward me, and I take one. I'm still not quite sure what to make of all this. I wonder how many other gods and goddesses there are in my world. But mostly I wonder if I really can control my dreams, if I can control my nightmares. And I think about that *voice*.

9

Dreaming men are haunted men.
STEPHEN VINCENT BENÉT

I don't want to sleep.

Sunday night. I stare at the clock. It's two in the morning. Tomorrow I have a test in English. Shakespeare. And I *need* to sleep. But I fear it.

I want to see Sebastian.

But I don't want to see Epiales.

So I listen to my iPod.

My cardio playlist thumps in my ears. I try to stay awake. I listen to Macklemore, "Can't Hold Us." Then this old song by Pearl Jam.

But then, despite blaring "Smile" by Eyedea & Abilities—my favorite song ever—my eyelids flutter.

I'm in a dance club. My favorite song is playing,
and I feel the beat deep in my belly because the music

is so loud and because I know the song so well that every note, every word, is part of my blood.

I have never been here before, so I feel lost and out of place. The club is dark, and the ceilings are very high. I can tell it is cavernous, even though I can't see much. It's the way the music bounces off the walls and the ceilings. A DJ, headphones to his ears, is perched above the crowd in a glass booth, with a huge red omega sign in fluorescent lights above him. Rich red velvet curtains hang from the walls and create private seating areas, making it impossible to look across the entire club. I feel claustrophobic, fenced in by velvet and body heat. A smoke machine has filled the place with gray mist. I reach out my hands, and my fingers disappear in the smoke. I can't see the floor.

Around me, people are gyrating and dancing to the bass. They are dressed in New York chic, black hipster clothes. One is more beautiful and good-looking than the next. They give off energy; the place seems to vibrate. It's also burning hot. I feel a breath on my neck and wheel around, startled.

Sebastian smiles.

"Miss me, Iris?" He leans in close and has to shout over the music.

I nod. But my feet feel frozen. I don't know what to say around him.

He stares at me. Then, slowly, he takes my hands, and we start dancing. I like the feel of my hand in his. His are strong and masculine. For some reason, I think of a sculptor's hands. Slightly rough, but powerful. Around us are so many other clubgoers that we're pressed together.

My heart pounds, only now it's not the rhythm making it thump, it's him. I rock to the beat— my song—and start to forget that anyone else is around us. To be dancing with him, to this song, feels amazing. We look into each other's eyes. I see forever there.

He leans down and pulls me closer still. My chest is pressed against his. It's only now I realize I'm wearing a black tank top, with just a hint of the lace of my favorite Victoria's Secret bra peeking out, and black skinny jeans, and I'm perched on some kick-ass heels. I feel sexy. He has on a black T-shirt that hugs him perfectly, and dark pants. The club is suffocating, and strands of my hair press against my cheeks; still my favorite song is playing and taking me somewhere higher, someplace I have never been before.

He takes his hands from mine and moves them to the sides of my throat, gently. I'm not afraid. He moves his hands into my hair, then pulls the curls up off my face and away from the back of my neck.

He leans down even closer, while still dancing, and blows softly on my neck where it's wet from the heat and dancing.

I shiver. I think I'm going to have a heart attack.

With my face in his hands, he looks me in the eyes, so far into me, I'm afraid my knees will buckle under me. Then, gently, he kisses my lips, so softly it's almost a breath at first. Then he nibbles, the slightest of tugs, on my lower lip. This kiss is like no other. I don't even know if we are dancing anymore, because all I feel is his chest pressed against me; all I hear is the music so loud in my ears, mingling with my heartbeat.

I kiss him back, my tongue flicking against his. He pulls me tighter to him. I feel our bodies meld together. I wrap my arms around his waist and move my hands up his back, feeling his muscles. His hands slide down to my jeans. I am lost in this kiss, like sinking deeper under the ocean.

And then I hear a screech. It's so high-pitched, I hear it above the music. He tenses, so I know he hears it, too.

Wrapping one arm around me, he lifts his head and scans the crowd. The thud-thud-thud of the music continues. I stand on tiptoe and peer over his shoulder, and I see we are surrounded by creatures. They seem human enough, but their faces look as if they've been rimmed with dark eyeliner, creating hollows and shadows beneath their eyes, which are iridescent black, like liquid mica.

The women are dressed like ravens, with flowing, shimmering black sleeves on their dresses, like wings, their hair sliced in sharp bobs. Three draw closer to us and bare their teeth behind wine-colored lipstick, exposing razor-sharp fangs.

"Vampires!" I scream.

Sebastian leans and kisses me again. He moves his mouth to my ear. "No. Keres. Time for you to go," he urges. "Tomorrow night, look for me behind our door. You'll feel it when you come to it. Trust yourself."

He pulls back and grabs my hand, and we run through the club toward the exit sign. Around us, everywhere, are writhing vampires. They hiss as we pass, steam rising off their bodies. The three vampires with the black-bobbed hair are chasing us, emitting the high-pitched shriek of strange, rabid animals. When we reach the emergency exit, its red letters sputtering, Sebastian opens the door; an alarm sounds as he pushes me through

∞

My alarm clock wakes me.

I stare at it. Six A.M.

Time for school.

I shut my eyes, wanting to feel that kiss. I touch my lips, wishing it were still happening, that he was here, with me. I wish it were real—minus the vampires.

I shake my head. Time for a shower. I feel as if I've been hit by a truck.

I get up and walk across the hall to my bathroom and start to brush my teeth. While I'm brushing, I glance in the mirror. My eyes widen.

I put my toothbrush down and stare at the back of my hand.

There, in red ink, is a mark. Made by a stamp like when you go to a club.

It's an omega sign.

*Dreams are symbolic in order that
they cannot be understood.*

CARL JUNG

think I pulled at least a B on my test. Shakespeare's
Midsummer Night's Dream. Annie meets me by my
locker, and we walk through the throngs of our high
school to the cafeteria, which is the usual madhouse.

"Look." She nudges me.

There, sitting by himself and reading a book, is
Henry Wu.

Annie—looking totally hot today in Rag & Bone
jeans and a cute sweater—smiles her biggest Annie-
all-American smile, wanders over, and plops into the
seat opposite him.

"Hi, Henry!"

I sit down next to her.

Henry Wu looks as if he might throw up his five hot dogs. His face is absolutely stricken.

"Hi, Annie. Hi, Iris." Although he says hello to me, he has eyes only for Annie.

She starts to question him like an investigator on *CSI*.

"So Henry, what are your plans for college?"

He blushes slightly: first his cheeks and then his neck flush, and then the color spreads to his chest, peeking between the edges of his navy polo shirt, where the top two buttons are undone. He looks down at his lunch tray. Then he takes a sip of Coke before clearing his throat and saying, "Um, Harvard."

"Interesting," Annie says. "Have any plans to, I don't know, do any sports there? Clubs?"

"I . . . um . . . row crew. We don't have a team here at school, but I belong to an athletic club with a team, and I . . . I was hoping . . . you know."

A little chill passes over me. *Just like Aphrodite said.* I look at Henry closely while they talk. Before Aphrodite, I just thought of him as some super-nerd, a nice super-nerd, but still. But now that I look at him, he's really good-looking; his eyes shimmer, his black hair is shiny, and his features are handsome.

And the way he looks at Annie . . . I wonder how we missed it all these years.

Annie is beautiful. Drop-dead. Any guy would fall for her—she's blond and athletic, and she has this creamy olive complexion from her mom's side of the family. But Henry Wu gazes across the table at her like she's the most perfect girl in the entire world—this world or the gods and goddesses one.

"Still playing soccer?" he asks. He clears his throat twice and nervously plays with the collar of his shirt.

Annie nods.

"Still volunteering at the camp for kids with cancer?"

Annie wrinkles her nose, perplexed. "Yeah. How did you know? Every summer for two weeks. I love it. But I don't tell anyone. My mom always taught me that you don't broadcast your good deeds. You just, you know, do them quietly."

"You mentioned it once about three years ago—in passing. On June third, when I asked what you were doing for the summer. You were going to be packing that night. You were hoping it would be cooler upstate. We were in the middle of a heat wave. The temperature was ninety-seven that day."

"Wow, Henry. I'm slightly freaked out by your

memory. But it's really cool that you remembered."

She stares at him, and I swear they have an honest-to-God—or as Aphrodite would say, honest-to-Zeus—moment. So I say, "I'm gonna run to the girls' bathroom. I'll be back in a few minutes." I mean, who am I to interfere with a soul-mate match?

I stand up and walk across the cafeteria, dodging a thrown napkin and Billy Kaye from the football team walking backward, not paying attention. When I look back at Henry and Annie, their heads are leaning across the table, and they're deep in conversation. She's using her hands when she talks, a sure sign she's happily excited. I feel my heart sort of go "aww." They are cute together.

I stroll down the hall to the girls' bathroom, walking around groups of kids milling near gray-green lockers, and I open the door. Oddly enough, despite it being lunchtime, the bathroom is completely empty. My footsteps echo as I walk across the floor. I look in the weird safety-glass mirror that I always think should be in a carnival funhouse and not a bathroom. As usual, the sinks are a mess, with crumbled brown paper towels on the floor, and wetness in the sinks themselves. The air reeks of cigarette smoke and the staleness of a bathroom with one tiny window that doesn't really open.

I find an open stall and shut the door. Then I hear someone walk in—actually, more than one someone—sets of heels along the black-and-white ceramic tiles. *Click-click-click*. *Click-click-click*. *Click-click-click*.

Which is kind of weird, since no one in our school really wears high heels. Except Ms. Peluso, the drama teacher, and Ms. Margarite, the Spanish teacher, who always wears these swirly skirts, very high heels, and black turtlenecks. I think it's because she's only four feet ten, and if she doesn't wear heels, she won't even be able to see over the kids in the halls.

But I know the heels do not belong to them. I feel it.

Then I hear some kind of hissing sound. Like from my dream last night.

And I get seriously freaked out. I peer through the crack around the edge of my stall door and see three goth-looking girls walking toward me. The three girls from the club. Girls? I mean freaks.

I glance down at the back of my hand again. The stamp is still there. I didn't wash it off because I needed to look at it today, to reassure myself that the kiss was real. That we have been together.

But if we were together and the kiss was real, then so are they.

I'm trapped. I peek through the crack again and look at them. They are beautiful, in this androgynous, unusual way, but scary-looking with black bobs, whitish foundation over airbrushed-perfect skin, and crimson lips. They have eyeliner drawn in a very dramatic way, extremely heavy, catlike and extended at the outer corners. Their eye makeup is smoky, and they're wearing some seriously thick false eyelashes beneath plucked high-arched brows. They are each wearing a skintight black leather dress—with a hemline so high that if our principal saw them, he would have a fit, considering our school dress code. Instant detention. "A skirt must reach at least one inch past a girls' fingertips when she has her hands flat at her sides." So says the school handbook. And Mr. Bentley stops girls in the hall for skirt patrol.

Only I am pretty sure these three don't care. And I know that they're not students. They're not even of this world. They would *mock* detention.

Or kill and eat everyone in it.

"Irissssssssssssssss," one says, her voice strangely metallic, "come out and play."

I try to swallow but have no spit. The sound of her voice feels like a cockroach just skittered up my spine. I look up at the ceiling. There's nowhere for me to go. I consider crawling *under* my stall walls into the stall next to mine—despite the fact that the bathroom floor of a school restroom is about as repulsive as you can get. But that won't help me. The window on the wall of the end stall is too small for me to squeeze out of, even if I wanted to try.

My cell phone. I pull it out of my back pocket. In the upper-left corner, it reads NO SERVICE. Our school is in a dead zone. Besides, whom would I call? I wouldn't want Annie to be in danger. And somehow 911 doesn't seem quite right. "Excuse me, but three vampires from my dream followed me back to reality."

I remember Aphrodite's words. That I'm powerful. I feel anything but. Didn't my mom say the Keres feast on human flesh? Or blood. Or something. *Think, Iris.* They are daughters of Nyx, so *technically* they're my aunts, and somehow they've been transported into my high school. It's them versus me. Yes, me, athletically challenged and new to the world of gods and goddesses. I don't know the rules. And I suspect that even if I did, the Keres don't play by them.

I wonder for a moment if I can reason with them. I was on the forensics debate team in ninth grade. We won the county championship. Reason with the Keres, though? I doubt it. Epiales didn't listen to reason. I'd love to explain to them that I can't control any of this. When I sleep, I always go to the hallway of many doors. And if they know a cure, I'm open to hearing it. I don't want this. I don't want this destiny. I don't want this birthright. So cure me. But I wonder if their cure is my death.

Click-click-click. I look up again, hoping for an answer, and I see one of them crawling across the *ceiling*. The ceiling. The rules of gravity and physics, the rules of the mortal world don't apply to them, not in the same way they apply to me, anyway. She stares down at me, her eyes colder than a snake's. She doesn't blink. She hisses, and her head skews at an odd angle, the way no human neck can. I silently pray Ms. Cannalloni, our gym teacher, will walk in right now to do one of her bathroom sweeps, looking for smokers. I picture Ms. C. flinging a dodgeball at the Keres on the ceiling.

But no one comes to my rescue.

I have to face them alone.

Find your power. I try to feel the kind of confidence I think Aphrodite has. Something stirs in the pit of my stomach, but mostly, I think it's an icy fear. Still.

I take a deep breath and open the stall door anyway, because I can't think of a single other thing to do.

"What do you want?" I say it with as much force and courage as I can muster while petrified.

They are identical. Triplets. One of them licks her lips. "We wanted to see you for ourselves. The filthy *half-breed*." The one on the ceiling leaps down, landing directly in front of me. Even if I wanted to make a break for the door, I can't now. She puts her face inches from mine and growls at me. Her breath smells like blood.

"Look," I exhale, then take a step backward. "I don't know *how* to stay out of the Underworld. If I did, I would. I promise you."

She grabs my wrist so fast, it's just a blur. Her fingers are icy as a corpse's. She pulls my wrist to her mouth. I fight her, pulling back. *Please don't bite me.*

She bares her fangs. The canine tips gleam, their points incredibly sharp.

She licks the inside of my wrist as I struggle to pull my hand away. Her tongue is cold, too. I see frost forming on my inner wrist.

I open my mouth to scream, thinking maybe someone will come.

Then the bathroom door opens and a gaggle of five or six girls walk in. They stop and stare.

As quickly as she grabbed my hand, the Keres

releases it. The three of them glare at me; their pupils open like cats' eyes. Then they turn on the heels of their six-inch blood-red stilettos, and *click-click-click* their way out of the bathroom.

"Who were *those* freaks?" asks Dari from my English class.

"I have no idea," I say, and roll my eyes. I walk to the sink, my hands shaking. I turn on the water and splash my face. I'm trying to act nonchalant . . . but inside? I know I was lucky this time. And that I have to learn how to control my dreams soon. Before something from the Underworld kills me.

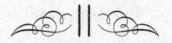

The interpretation of dreams is the royal road to a knowledge of the unconscious activities of the mind.

SIGMUND FREUD

Annie and I wait in the reception area of Dr. Koios's office. It's Christmas break. I have survived my last exam today. But my dreams? I'm not so sure.

Suddenly, now that my eyes have been opened to gods and goddesses among us, I see the clues. On the shelves of the waiting room are pieces of pottery that I'm sure are ancient shards—authentic pieces from the Byzantine era or something. My mom would go crazy for this stuff. A single black-and-white photograph is framed on the wall opposite the couch where Annie and I are sitting. *Most* doctors would have their degrees matted and behind glass. Instead, his photograph is of the Greek isles, a bleached white house overlooking a clear sea. A potted palm sits in the corner, and a white-noise machine drones.

The door opens, and he escorts out a patient and then smiles when he sees Annie and me.

"So long, Carol . . ." He waves her off. The woman departs.

"Come on in, girls."

We walk in, and both of us sit down on his leather couch.

We stare at him.

"Yes, now, ready for your next hypnosis session, Iris?"

"Not so fast," I say. I unravel my scarf and shake out my black peacoat.

"Oh?" He raises an eyebrow. "You have more questions?"

"You could say that," Annie offers. Her coat is already draped across her lap.

"We went to see Aphrodite." I say it aloud and let the words hang in the air between us.

He doesn't so much answer, more like he exhales an "Oh," his lips forming a perfect circle.

"So when were you going to tell me?" I ask accusingly.

He sits down behind his desk and spreads his palms

out flat on the wooden surface. He has a bust of a Greek god—I'm guessing Zeus—on the shelf directly behind him. How had I missed the clues?

"So many people end up worshipping their therapist. They view them as superhuman. How does one go about telling a patient that he is, in fact, superhuman?"

His eyes are moist and kindly. I smile because I sense I can trust him in the same way I felt in an instant that I could trust Aphrodite. "Point taken. But now that I know who you really are, can you help me?"

"Why don't we start with your telling me what's really going on? I could sense you were holding back from me—*withholding* in therapy lingo."

"How does one go about telling her therapist that things from her dreams are following her back to real life? If I had told you—before I knew you were a god and all—you would have had me committed."

"Touché! Can we speak frankly now?"

I nod.

"All right, Iris. From now on no secrets between us. Spill it."

Annie glances at me. She's still upset about the Keres—I had told her about them once I returned to the lunchroom. I look at Dr. Koios. I bite the inside of my cheek. It all feels so huge.

He stands up from behind his desk and comes over and sits down on the coffee table, so our knees practically touch. He looks me in the eyes. "I can't help you if you don't trust me."

So I start at the beginning. Not the vines on my leg, but the *very* beginning, with my mother and Morpheus and my strange parentage, and then with my dreams, going as far back as I can remember. I tell him about the voice, the voice of my protector in that world. My dream guardian, according to my mom. I tell him about how—under hypnosis—I finally got to see him. I tell him about the club— leaving out the kiss. That's private. I take him all the way through to today.

"Very interesting," he says, tapping his index fingers together.

"Well," Annie asks, "can you help her?" She exhales. "*Please?*" Her eyes are filled with best-friend worry.

He nods.

"Well, first, when you are in the Underworld— your dream world—you're still in charge. That is what lucid dreaming is."

"But I don't feel in charge."

"You are. It's *your* dream world. You must try to pay attention to the voice."

"I do."

"No, not *his* voice. Your subconscious voice. Your *own* voice."

"I don't have any idea what you mean," I whine.

"Have you ever had a nightmare during which you were incredibly upset, but while you were in the *middle* of the nightmare, you heard your own voice, perhaps advising you to *stop* the nightmare? That little voice going 'Wake up, wake up'? Maybe you even felt in a world between the nightmare and waking—you were aware you were thrashing, you knew it was a nightmare. But you were still in its grips."

I think about it. "Ye-ah," I finally say.

"That is lucid dreaming. The dreamer controls the dream, not vice versa."

"I still don't understand. Even if I know I'm dreaming, I'm still in the dream world."

"People who lucid dream can change the ending."

"Really?"

"Yes. Let me give you an example. Chase dreams are extremely common. They usually symbolize stresses chasing the dreamer, phobias, or times when life gets overwhelming. Have you ever had one?"

I nod and look at Annie.

"Sure," she says. "Like, I'm pretty sure everyone does."

"Have you had one that was terrifying? Truly terrifying, heart pounding?"

Again, we both nod.

He smiles. "The lucid dreamer will stop that dream. She'll turn around and say, 'Why are you chasing me?' And that simple act usually stops the dream, stops the pattern."

"Okay. So I know I lucid dream," I say. "Maybe that comes with being Morpheus's daughter, too. But *controlling* it? I don't think I could do that."

"Yes, you can."

"How?"

"It's training. That's where I come in. I'll be here with you. I'll teach you how. You just need to be aware."

Easy for him to say. "Have you met Epiales?" I ask him.

He coughs slightly. "Ahem . . . um . . . well . . ."

"I'll take that as a firm yes."

"Fine. Epiales is . . . rather . . . difficult. Do you know the history of the Underworld?"

"No," I admit. "I'm still trying to get up to speed with who's who." So many gods, and they're all related in odd ways. It's impossible to keep them straight unless you're part of their family. Even if you are part of their family.

"Hades is the brother of Zeus. At one time there was a great war. It lasted a decade. At the end of which, Hades, Zeus, and another brother, Poseidon, drew lots to divide up the world—all of the world both seen and unseen. Zeus got to rule the skies from Mount Olympus, Poseidon drew all of the seas, and Hades is king of the Underworld. He's got a bad marriage, among other things. And the Underworld is a complicated and strange and murky place. On the fringes of the Underworld is the land of dreams, the land of Night. Morpheus, Hypnos, Nyx, and Epiales, and their kind all exist between Zeus's kingdom and the Underworld. An in-between place—one where they are beholden to both Zeus and Hades. Morpheus is closer to Zeus, and Epiales to Hades. Death and nightmares are closely entwined, after all. However, all of the realms are in delicate balance. Death must exist. Hades is not evil—he exists to maintain balance with Zeus and Poseidon. Just as Epiales is the balance to Morpheus. But . . . he is extremely difficult to control. And becoming less so by the century. He is a fearsome enemy."

"Wonderful," I groan.

"That does not mean you cannot fight him, Iris.

But to do so, you'll need to dream lucidly."

"Can I ask you something?" I hesitate.

"No secrets in here. Not anymore. Ask."

"You and Aphrodite exist here. And Epiales, he's shown up in the real world. Can Sebastian come into this world? Could I bring him back?" I think of what Aphrodite said, about crossing the realms.

"He can. By crossing the River of Sorrows. And, of course, in doing that, he gives up his immortality."

Annie and I exchange glances.

"What?" Annie asks.

"Aphrodite didn't mention that," I add.

"Well, I guess she thought it was obvious."

I look at him. "Let me get this straight . . . Aphrodite gave it all up to be a matchmaker? You gave up immortality to be a Jersey hypnotherapist?"

"Yeah, I love to work with Snooki."

"Get out!" Annie shrieks and slaps his knee.

He rolls his eyes. "Of course not. But yes. I age slower than most humans, but I am mortal. One day I will die. But here I think I make a difference. My existence has great purpose."

"And you're sure you can teach me to beat Epiales?" I ask.

"I can teach you to lucid dream. You control your destiny in the dream world, Iris. Are you ready?"

I look at Annie. She nods and reaches over to give my hand a squeeze.

"I think so."

"All right. Just like before, I'm going to lead you into deep relaxation. But this time, I'm going to lead you down the hallway of many doors intentionally. And you are in control."

"What am I supposed to do?"

"Listen for my voice. When I see you're in trouble, like last time, when you were thrashing around, I will lead you out. You *must* listen to me. Okay? That's part of the deal."

I nod.

"All right then. Come over to the chair and get comfortable. Annie can stay here on the couch."

"She's making sure you don't hypnotize me naked." I wink.

Dr. Koios rolls his eyes, and a smile dances across his lips. "You girls are ridiculous. And delightful. Now, come sit and close your eyes."

I move to the comfortable armchair with the ottoman and sink down into it. I shift until I am really comfy. I shut my eyes. Then I pop them open.

"So Sebastian said to meet him in our special place behind our door or . . ." I try to remember. "He said . . . something about knowing where it is.

Trusting myself. But I don't have any idea where it is or what it could be."

Dr. Koios kneels down so he's looking me directly in the eyes. "In the Underworld, the dream world, you need to trust your instincts. Before when you dreamed, it felt as if things happened *to* you. Now when you go, you must remember that you are the dreamer. You can control what happens. You have the power, Iris. You are Morpheus's daughter. In the history of mankind, there has never been another."

That word again. *Power*. I hear what he's saying, but I have no idea what to do or how to do it. I also can't help but think, wow, in all eternity, Morpheus has never loved another woman. Just my mom. That's better than a sperm donor from Mensa.

"Okay," I whisper. I look at Annie. She winks and gives me a thumbs-up.

I shut my eyes.

I hear Dr. Koios's voice.

"With each inhale, relax into the chair. With each exhale, you will relax, deeper and deeper. Inhale into deep relaxation. Feel all the tension and stress leave your body and float away. Exhale into deep relaxation as your cares leave you. Your muscles are no longer tense. You are melting into the chair."

His voice is calming, soothing, and I feel myself relaxing and drifting away, like floating on a raft in a pool.

Only this time, as I start to float away, to feel sleepy and deeply relaxed, I hear Dr. Koios's voice.

"You now will enter the hallway of many doors."

In my mind, I turn around.

I am in the long, dark hallway of many doors. The key ring and keys are in my right hand. They jingle, and the brass ring feels chilly in my palm.

I walk past a door painted blacker than the darkest night. I shudder. Who would enter a black door? But carved on it is a pair of swans. I linger for a moment, captivated by the swans. But the door seems to breathe, to vibrate as if it were alive. The blackness is so dark it threatens to suck me in. It is liquidlike, endless somehow.

I walk on. The hallway has hundreds of doors on my left and on my right. They seem to stretch into infinity. I pass one that is painted a deep shade of red, lacquered to a sheen so polished I can see my faint reflection in it. But this door does not call to me.

I keep thinking of the black door, even as I pass a tall door inlaid with gold. And then one that looks like it's from some baroque palace.

From far away, I hear a voice. I know this voice.

"Trust your instincts, Iris. Annie and I are here for you."

I am back in the hallway. I am safe. For now. But it's dark. I shut my eyes, exhale, then open them and look behind me, and for the first time, there are sconces on the walls, illuminating my way. I just walked there. How can there now be flames offering a comforting light? Did I just make them materialize? But I smile and am grateful for the light, flickering and dancing on the walls; I'm not going to ask questions. For the first time, I notice the walls are made of stone, weathered and ancient. I reach out my left hand and touch the stone. The wall is smooth, like polished rock, and cool.

I look ahead of me. The sconces stretch as far as my eye can see, even as the tunnel feels like an endless maw. But for some reason, I don't think our special place is in front of me. Instead, I turn around and head back where I came from to find the black door again. I don't know why this one door, of all the others, draws me to it. Trust your instincts. Is this the special place?

The two swans are intricately carved. Their necks are entwined. The male swan is slightly larger, and the female swan rests her head against him. They are

*mated for life. I know this deep down, even though
I have never seen this door before.*

*I feel a throbbing in my belly. The way I feel when
I hear Sebastian's voice. I put my hand on the door.
It vibrates like a pulse.*

But what about the key?

*I look down at my key ring. Hundreds of keys.
How will I know which one will open this particular
door?*

*I lift up the ring to the light of a sconce. I touch
them, running my fingers over all the keys until one
feels hot. I single it out and hold it closer to the
flame. This is the key. I know it. There is a feather
carved on it.*

*I insert the key into the lock, and it slides in
perfectly. I turn it and hear the click.*

Holding my breath, I open the door and enter.

I smile.

*I am in the Metropolitan Museum of Art. This is
our special place?*

*I love museums. And all my life I have wanted to
stroll through one, hand in hand with someone I love,
like I have seen so many others do. Sophisticated
and very Manhattan-like. It's always seemed like the
most romantic thing in the world to me, to wander
aimlessly among the masterpieces.*

I walk up to a bronze cast of Rodin's The Thinker.

I stare at it. No one else is in the museum. No security guards. No other people. The room is cavernous and completely silent, except for the sounds of my own breathing. I reach out and caress the surface of the sculpture, which is smooth, the muscles of the biceps well defined, elbow resting on knee. No alarm goes off. No security guard comes. I smile. This is very cool.

I walk around the thinking man made of bronze, and there he is. As if he's been waiting for me.

Sebastian.

"What took you so long?"

I grin. "I needed to find the right door."

"Come with me." He extends his hand.

When I take it, my insides quiver. He is dressed in jeans and a white oxford-cloth shirt, the top two buttons undone so I see the curve of his collarbone. He smells like the sea, somehow.

We walk, hand in hand, through the museum, wandering quietly. We don't really talk. It's almost like we're in a church. To speak would ruin it. From time to time, we stop in front of a painting, and he moves to stand behind me, wrapping both his arms around my waist, my head leaning back against his chest. He kisses my neck, or smells my hair. It seems we like the same paintings. We never say to each other at which ones we should stop, and yet it always seems as if we pause at the same moment, captivated by the same things. We stand in front of Vincent van Gogh's painting of sunflowers, their golden color against a blue background. It has always been my favorite, and I have a print of it hanging on the wall of my bedroom.

"Your favorite," he murmurs. He lifts my hand to his lips and kisses the inside of my wrist, his tongue flicking it for just a fraction of a second.

But suddenly, I'm angry. I pull my hand away.

"It isn't fair."

He wrinkles his forehead, eyes concerned. "What isn't fair?"

"You know everything about me. You've been in my head and in my dreams for as long as I can remember. You know that I love this painting. What else do you know about me?" I ask this as an accusation. Annie seems to be getting a normal boyfriend—why can't I have one?

"I know that you're afraid of clowns." He smirks and tries to take my hand.

I pull it away.

"Look, they freak me out. It is a perfectly legitimate fear." I narrow my eyes, my heart pounding. I try to calm down, but I can't.

"Iris." His voice is gentle. "I know that you used to complain about your grandfather making you *go to museums, but that secretly you loved it. That your time with him made you feel special . . . I know you love the Yankees because of him, and when you should have been studying your spelling words in third grade, you were memorizing their batting order so you could impress him. But I also know you never needed to do anything to impress him because he loves you so extraordinarily. You are his sun and his moon. I know that when your grandmother died, he stopped going to church. And you became his reason to go on. You are his prayer. Or the answer to one."*

My eyes well. I turn my head because I don't want him to see my tears. He knows enough about my vulnerabilities. I'm still mad. Just maybe a little less so.

"I know that the only person who has ever seen you cry over your mother is Annie. I know that every time you have received an award—like the time your short story won the county contest and you had a reading at the library—Annie has sat in the front row next to your grandfather. Sometimes with her mother, even though Mrs. Casey has six children and no free time. I know that your heart would still feel a pang because that seat should have been where your mother sat. But that you knew somehow her illness wasn't fair. You never complained, especially to your grandfather, because to do so would have meant you were saying to him that all his love was not enough."

I want him to stop. It's too painful that he can speak truths I don't even acknowledge to myself. I want to dream him away. Hide. But my feet are rooted to the floor. There is no hiding from him.

"I know that this scar"—he reaches out and touches the tiny pale scar in the shape of a sunburst by my left eye—"is from when you fell from the tree house. I know that to me"—he tilts my head until I am looking into his eyes—"that little imperfection makes you even more perfect."

"But . . ." I pause to collect my voice. "I know nothing about you. And that's not fair. You've been in my head. This voice. And how can you be . . . my age? But then you were the boy in the tree house? How can you change like that?"

"I am everything you need me to be. I am your guardian in the dreamworld. Just like in a dream you can change from six to sixteen inside of a breath, so can I. Just as you can fly or make sconces appear on the wall, so can I be what you need me to be. It is my world. This world."

His index finger caresses my scar. I smell the ocean on him. His eyes dilate. His lashes are black and thick. But I shut my eyes for a moment. "I don't even know if you're real. And I won't be my mother. I will not. . . ."

I let the words drift away. I open my eyes again. I

will not fall in love with someone who can't be a part of my world. My real world. How much of her life has she wasted in sleep? I know she loves Morpheus, but really? A few stolen moments in twenty years? I can't do it. I am not that girl.

"I will tell you about me, then." He smiles. "Everything you want to know."

We walk on to the Degas exhibit, ballerinas in tutus at the barre.

"I was born in the dreamworld of Hypnos, Epiales, and Morpheus, with my allegiance to your father. But the way I was born is not the way you were born. I was part of the dreamworld. I was born of the figment of your imagination, the spark of a child who needed a protector from her nightmares."

I stop.

"No," I breathe. What he is telling me cannot be possible. I feel nauseous. "I made you up?"

"You are very powerful, Iris."

That word again. Powerful.

"I've spent my life in your dreams."

"But you have no mother or father? You've never been to school?" I almost laugh because I know the questions are ridiculous. His life has been nothing like mine. I remember the dream, the tree-house dream. One moment he was a little boy. The next he was the guy standing in front of me. The man.

He shakes his head. "No. My world is the hallway, behind those doors, those endless doors. My voice was the one telling you to run in dreams when you were in danger. I was protecting you. From Epiales. My world is you, Iris."

I swallow. "Why does my uncle hate me so much?"

"You have the power of a demi-goddess. But you have a mortal life. You laugh. You cry. You bleed. You . . . love. You have what he can never have: the power of the gods and the power of the mortal world, all in one."

I touch his arm, as if to reassure myself that he's here. "I couldn't have just dreamed you up." He's too perfect.

His cheeks flush. "You were the spark, but just the spark. I was born into the netherworld, on the fringes of the Underworld, with the beasts that go bump in the night . . . and the worlds behind the doors that make you feel as if you must be in heaven. And until you finally found me, I assumed I would stay here forever."

"And now?"

He looks away. "I would like to come to your world. With you. In your waking life."

"But that would mean you lose your immortality. I couldn't let you do that, Sebastian."

I think of my grandfather. Someday he's going to

die. Just the thought of it, just for a second, when I'm alone in my room, will make me dizzy. I would give anything for him to be immortal. But the times he's spoken about getting old, he's only said that he'll be happy to be with my grandmother again and that he hopes she's making a big pot of gravy because he's tired of takeout.

"Immortality is not necessarily a gift. Humans only think it is."

He comes close to me, until we're standing chest to chest. A tear escapes my eye, and he leans down and kisses it. His scent makes my head spin. He moves his mouth to mine and nibbles my bottom lip, then runs his tongue along it, feather soft, before kissing me fiercely. I kiss him back, and then put my hands in his hair, wrapping them in his curls. He slides one arm around me at the small of my spine, as if it were somehow possible to pull me into him, to entwine us like the swans. He takes his other hand and slowly moves it under my shirt, until he is cupping my breast. He presses against it, and then I feel his finger tracing the center of my breastbone up to the hollow between my collarbone. I feel as if I can't breathe, as if the museum has disappeared and we are the only two souls in the entire universe.

And then I hear it. That pounding. We both open our eyes at once. I don't know how long we've been here. It has felt like an entire day. But I think Epiales's minions have found us.

"You have to go." Sebastian slides his hand out, pulling away from me, his breath ragged. I see the slightest of tremors in his hands. And I know it's not because he's afraid, but because of us—because of me. I have that effect on him. And that makes me happy. Because he does that to me, too. I don't want this dream to end. Not like this. Not again.

I shake my head. "No. It's my dream. I control it."

I hear Dr. Koios's voice. "Iris, it's time for you to come out of your dream. You must come back to us now."

Not yet. I steal one more kiss from him. A deep kiss, as if it's the last kiss I will ever have with him. The last kiss of my entire life. "Aphrodite says you must cross the River of Sorrows to exist in my world, but I can't let you do it. Stay here. Promise me. Stay here, and I will keep finding you. Now that I know how. Now that we have"—I search for the word— "this connection. It will be easier."

Easier, I think. Nothing about this is easy. And always there is the threat of Epiales.

"No!" he says furiously.

I look at Sebastian, my protector. My personal

guardian. "I would come here for you, every night," I whisper, even as I hear the words and know what that would mean. I would sleep. Like my mother.

He puts his hands on my shoulders. "You don't want to be like your mother and Morpheus. All of the Underworld, all of the dreamworld, the Olympians, they all know how he aches for her. He mourns her when she is not here. But if he leaves his throne for her, if he makes that sacrifice, then Epiales will take his crown. The balance will be destroyed. There will be no more dreams, only darkness. The human world will be rendered in nightmares."

I think of what that would mean. If there was no more peaceful sleep, if every night people had only the most horrid of nightmares. But before I can ask more questions, from far off in the museum, I hear deep voices.

Next, the sounds of footfalls, like many men running on the marble floors.

"Iris . . . you must come back to Annie and me now."

"Please, Iris," Annie's voice begs me. "Please, come back. Right now."

I look around. I don't see an exit. The room we are in is actually an anteroom. Our only choice is to go into the main hall, and there we'll be easy to spot. I start to panic. But then I remember. This is my dream, and I have the power.

Holding hands, we step into the main concourse. I see thirty or forty men, dressed like soldiers, running toward us from the far end of the museum. I grab Sebastian's hand. I know Dr. Koios says I can stop and ask someone why he's chasing me, but in my gut, I have a feeling that this is not the time. Not here, not in this dream.

"Run!" I say to him. We race through the museum. We run left, then right, through exhibits and rooms full of priceless art. It's a giant maze. Every time I think we have reached a room that might buy us freedom, I am deceived. We run from room to room, portraits of gods and goddesses, kings and chiefs, maidens and lions, soldiers and farmers a blur of oil on canvas. We pass sunsets and flowers, marble busts and gold-inlaid drinking vessels. But it's a dizzying array, and behind me, I hear the voices of our pursuers gaining on us.

"There's no escape," Sebastian shouts. "We're trapped!"

We turn a corner. We are in the great hall of antiquities. All around us are ancient mummies and statues of civilizations long fallen. We cannot go back the way we came. The soldiers are coming.

"Come on," I yell. This is my dream. Sebastian and I duck behind a stone sarcophagus in the corner. We crouch down. Soldiers enter the hall. My heart thumps, and I think they will hear its beat alone. But their footsteps pass us, and they run on to the next exhibit.

Follow me, I mouth. We creep from behind the sarcophagus and tiptoe across the hall. But as we move into the open, a soldier retraces his steps and spots us.

"They're here!"

Sebastian pulls me behind a tall stone statue of a Roman god. As we take cover, I hear the sounds of gunfire, so loud and so close my ears ring. A bullet ricochets off the statue we're behind, taking a chunk of the stone god's face off. I feel chips of stone strike my face. Dust stings my eyes.

The soldiers are closer. More bullets echo in the hall. A glass case containing ancient pottery shatters near us, spraying me with shards, but I have no time to react.

This is getting way too close—and too real—for comfort.

No, I can do this. I control my dream.

I grab Sebastian's hand, and we run straight toward a wall. I shout, "Trust me." Neither one of *us hesitates. And as we near the stone wall, at the last possible second, a door appears with an exit sign above it. I created the door.*

Boom! *I push down on the brass handle.*

And Sebastian and I burst through into blinding sunlight.

I blink my eyes. I try to look around the room, but my eyes hurt too much. "Can you dim that light?" I ask Dr. Koios weakly. I know Sebastian is not with me. I am here.

And he is there.

Dr. Koios nods. "Annie, go over to that credenza there and pour her a glass of water."

Annie's face is pale. Her eyes are wide. She does as he asks, and he switches off the light near me so his office is illuminated only by the soft green glow of a banker's lamp on his desk.

Annie pours water from a glass decanter into a tumbler and brings it to me. Her hand is shaking, and the water spills slightly over the side of the glass.

I take the glass from her and gratefully gulp down a huge sip. My throat is parched. "Thanks. I'm okay."

Dr. Koios looks very worried. As worried as Annie. "I don't know about okay." His voice is somber.

I look at him quizzically. He stands and walks to the wall by his desk, taking down a small mirror. He returns to my side and hands it to me.

Nervously, I take it and look at my reflection. There are tiny cuts on my right cheek—from where the shards hit me.

"Ho-ly crap." I exhale. No wonder Annie is so shaken.

Both of them sit on the couch opposite me.

"It was like *The Exorcist*," Annie says. "The cuts appeared on your face right in front of us."

"Tell me exactly what happened," Dr. Koios commands. "Everything."

I do. Leaving out the part about Sebastian feeling me underneath my T-shirt. I figure that little detail can stay in my head.

"I made the door appear. I did it." I hear in my voice how proud I am. I really did it. I controlled my dream.

"But if you hadn't . . ." He shakes his head. "Iris, I'm worried for your safety. You could have been injured. Or killed."

"But it's only a dream, right? You said so yourself. You said I control it. And I did!"

"No, well . . . How do you feel right now?"

Now that I think about it, I hurt. "Really exhausted. Like when I have the flu or something." It's true. My muscles ache so much they're throbbing.

Dr. Koios's face is grim. "Iris, if you were an ordinary person having a lucid dream, then yes. If you're hurt in a dream, or killed, it's just a dream. But this is different. First of all, it's not entirely unheard of for people to die in their sleep. There have been cases of older persons having a literal heart attack from the stress in their nightmares, although it's exceedingly rare. But you are *not* an ordinary person. Your father is the great god Morpheus. Every dream a human has ever dreamed from the dawn of time, he has controlled, along with the vast numbers of citizens of the Underworld who do his bidding in those dreams. And *you* are his daughter." He pauses, taking a deep breath.

"Iris, after seeing you dream just now, I don't think it's as simple as lucid dreaming. I have never encountered this before. Even I am on shaky ground, uncharted territory. It's not just your uncle following you into reality. You bring back artifacts from your dreams. My fear—my terrible and unimaginable fear, my dear, dear Iris—is that if you are injured or killed in your dream, that . . ."

He lets his words trail off.

I think of nearly being bitten by one of the Keres. I think of the guns those soldiers carried. I think of the bullets ricocheting off the museum walls. It was a dream. But it was real.

I touch my cheek. I feel the blood droplets. I stare at Dr. Koios as what he is saying sinks in.

My dreams might kill me.

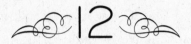

12

Yes: I am a dreamer. For a dreamer is one who can only find his way by moonlight, and his punishment is that he sees the dawn before the rest of the world.

OSCAR WILDE

Annie drives me home. Dr. Koios makes an appointment with me for three days from now. He says I need more training. I need to build on my power. He says to try to avoid the hallway of my dreams until then. To try not to sleep too much. Since I am an insomniac, that shouldn't be much of a problem.

Annie doesn't talk in the car. Not one word the whole way. I'm too exhausted to speak, so we listen to her iPod plugged into the car stereo. I lean my head against the window, wishing the aching in my legs and arms would stop. Then, as we pull onto Main Street, "our" song comes on.

It's completely dorky, but we have a whole Annie and Iris playlist. Every year it grows with new favorite songs—everything from rap to rock to indie to pop. But one is special. When we were in seventh grade, Mr. and Mrs. Casey took us to see *Wicked* on Broadway for Annie's birthday, and then we went out for dinner to this restaurant that served the most amazing paella—her favorite dish. Ever since seeing that musical, "Defying Gravity" has been *our* song.

She makes a right and pulls down a side street, then drives down the hill to the riverfront. We used to come here and sit and look at the water until they built this tall condo building that obscures the view. Like the world needs more condos. She parks the car, and when she turns to look at me, she's crying a little. She sometimes gets this way when "Defying Gravity" plays while she has PMS, but I don't think that's it this time.

"Iris, you can't keep going there." She sniffles.

"Annie. I don't know how *not* to go there. At least not yet."

"Dr. Koios can teach you." She's silent for a minute. When she speaks again, her voice is thin and hollow. "I can't lose you. This is really scaring me, and I can't even talk to anyone. I can't tell my parents. I can't tell another living soul. For God's sake, Iris, *I'm* going to need therapy with Dr. Koios to get over this trauma!"

I give her this little smirk and try to get her not to worry. "Annie—"

"Don't 'Annie' me," she playfully scolds. But then she turns serious again, eyes still filled with tears. "You know that I wouldn't want to talk to anyone about this anyway, because *you're* the person I tell everything to. Everything. And if something happens to you, I will never, ever get over it."

I reach out and grab her hand. "Oh, Annie, you know I love you, too." I try to imagine how I would feel if the situation was reversed. Without my mom around much, Annie and her family mean the world to me. She's like my sister. We're closer than sisters. We finish each other's sentences. We know what the other thinks before she even thinks it. I know if it was the other way around, I would tell her to stop going to the land of dreams.

She exhales. "I know I'm being selfish. But I wish you would stay away from Sebastian."

I bite the inside of my cheek. Now that I've found him, found the man who matches the voice, do I just give him up? How can I?

She shakes her head. "I just don't see how this will end well. This isn't some movie or book where someone can just write you a happy ending, Iris. He's . . . he's not even *human*. That's not like dating someone who's a different race or religion—like I would care about that, like anyone *should* care about that. It's not like dating someone a few years older. It's not even like dating a bad boy who might not be good for you. Sebastian doesn't even live in the same *world* as you. And I don't want to see you end up like your mom. I'm sorry, but . . ."

I know she doesn't mean to hurt me. It's true. I don't want to end up like my mom, either.

"Just answer me something." She stares right at me.

"What?" I say quietly.

"Do you love him?"

I don't answer right away. I think about it. How can I love someone I barely know? But . . . this is different somehow. Because in some other way, he's a part of me. He's been the voice, my protector, my guardian, for so long now. He's been with me, that voice, that angel in my sleep, every night. *Every* night—well, except for the ones when I don't sleep. And deep down, I have always known.

"I . . . haven't said the words. Not to him."

"But has he said them to you?"

I shake my head. I'm quiet for a minute or two.

"You know Carl Jung? The archetypes?"

Annie nods. "Don't even say it. He's your soul mate, isn't he?"

"I think so." Even though I say I *think* so, I know it. Just talking about it out loud with Annie confirms it in my gut.

"I have to tell you something, Iris."

"What?"

"Henry Wu . . . we definitely had a 'moment,' at lunch."

"Would you have had it if Aphrodite hadn't told you about your future?"

"I don't know. I certainly wouldn't have sat down with him at the table in the first place. I wouldn't have been curious about him at all. He would have been plain old Henry Wu, supergenius. So maybe it wouldn't have happened until we were twenty-six, like she said. But now that I have . . . Henry Wu, sweet, *adorable*, beanpole Henry Wu . . . he makes my insides wobble."

I laugh.

"I wanted to grab his face and kiss him right there." She mimics the motion, since she's fundamentally incapable of talking without using her hands. "Then he'd think I was completely nuts." She makes a whirling motion with her fingers near her temple, and she crosses her eyes.

"Great. Once he gets to know you, then he can find out you really *are* nuts."

She's not crying anymore, but she's laughing so hard at the ridiculousness of it all that tears are running down her face. Happy tears.

"I guess what I'm saying," she says, wiping her sleeve across her face, "is if he's your soul mate, if he really is, then you need to be with him. We just have to find a way to do it so you're safe. And you don't become your mom." She touches my cheek where I have a cut. It stings a little. "And we'll figure it out together. Like we always have. Everything from boys to trig."

I love my bestie.

"Promise me you'll listen to Dr. Koios and follow his instructions, though. That you'll come back to us when he tells you to."

"I promise."

She holds up her pinkie. "Pinkie promise."

"We haven't made a pinkie promise since fourth grade when—"

"When we promised to be maid of honor at each other's weddings."

I lift up my hand. I lock my pinkie with hers.

"Promise."

She leans across the car and hugs me. "All right, let's get home. I'm starving."

She puts the car into drive, and we zoom up the hill and to my house.

"Want to stay for dinner?" I ask.

"Can we do sushi takeout?"

I nod. "I'm sure Grandpa would be up for that. He likes eel. And California rolls. And we haven't had sushi takeout in a whole week and a half. Last night was Mexican."

"I'm so craving a spider roll." She turns off the engine, and we climb out of the car. "Have you gotten your Christmas tree yet?"

"Sunday night. We always go to that lot at the top of the hill by the hospital. We've still got to pull the decorations down from the attic, though."

We walk up the front steps. I move to open the door, but I see it's already open a crack. I swing the door wide, and then I scream. Annie is right behind me as we rush into the house.

The living room is a disaster, with picture frames broken and glass on the carpet. The couch is on its side. The desk has had all its drawers pulled out, and there are papers and rubber bands and paper clips all over the place.

"Grandpa?" I call out, panic rising with bile in my throat. I run from the living room down the hall, calling for him. "Grandpa! Mom!" And I see my mom's bedroom door is open.

Annie calls out, "Iris! Don't. The burglars could still be here. I'll call nine-one-one!"

"*No! Don't!*" I scream over my shoulder. "It's not burglars. It's that bastard Epiales. I know it!"

I run into my mom's room. The IV pole we have for her is on the floor, and her sheets are torn off. The pictures of the two of us taped to her dresser have been torn into pieces. Her bed is empty.

I run to my room.

"Oh my God," I whisper.

On my mirror, in lipstick, someone has written:

COME FIND THEM

Epiales has kidnapped my mother and grandfather.

13

You know that place between sleep and awake, the place where you can still remember dreaming? That's where I'll always love you. That's where I'll be waiting.

HOOK, 1991

I collapse into a sitting position onto my bed and pull one of the pillows against my chest. My heart shatters.

I start to cry, the tears coming from the place in my soul that has always somehow known I was different, a fatherless girl. The place where I feel an ache for what I am. For who I am, for the whole confusing mess of my birthright. And I cry for my mom and Grandpa, the two people I love most in the world. Annie sits next to me and just puts her arms around me until I can't cry anymore. She pats my back.

"Shh, Iris. I promise. We'll get them back. We'll call the police and . . ."

I pull away and look at her. "I can't call the police. What am I going to say? A psychotic *god* with mirrored eyes took her? I can't even tell your mom and dad. I don't know what to do. I have to pretend that everything is okay until I can figure this out."

She stands up and goes into the bathroom and gets me a roll of toilet paper so I can blow my nose and dry my face.

"You can't stay here alone, Iris. It's too dangerous. Come stay at my house for a few days. Christmas break is here. We'll tell my parents . . . hmm." She crinkles her face. "We'll tell them that your grandfather took your mom to the Mayo Clinic or something. That they had a cancellation and he and your mom took it. And that you need to stay with us. Wouldn't want you alone at the holiday time."

I shake my head. "I appreciate it, Annie. But I'm not putting your family in danger."

"You would do it for me."

"I know. But your parents have been like my substitute parents practically since we've met. I won't do that. What if something happened to them, or to you, or to the Tiny Terrors? I'd never forgive myself."

My only family members in this whole wide *real* world are gone. And Annie's right, I can't stay here, waiting for my deranged uncle to come snatch me, too. And if I can't go to my only other "family," what am I going to do? And then it dawns on me. I *have* another family member.

I lean over and open my desk drawer and dig around.

"Aphrodite's card," I say, holding it up.

Annie's face brightens. "Brilliant! Call her. Do you think she'll come stay with you?"

"I hope so. She *is* my aunt, after all. But . . . I've only met her that once, and she might not want to get involved." I think of Epiales. Of his dead voice and insane eyes. I don't know if anyone would want to go up against him if she didn't have to.

With a shaking hand, I dial her number.

I get her voice mail. "You have reached the private phone line of Aphrodite Cypris, Matchmaker to the Stars. Want to find the love of your life? Then leave a message at the beep."

I take a deep breath. Then I speak. "Aphrodite? *Aunt* Aphrodite . . . I'm in trouble. Big trouble. This is Iris, by the way. Um . . . I came home from a session with Dr. Koios, and my house was ransacked—and my grandfather and mother have been taken. I know it was Epiales, and I know they're in grave danger. I don't know what to do, or where to turn. I'm sorry to bother you. Really sorry. But I need help, and I don't know who else to call. Please call me back."

I disconnect the call and look at Annie and shrug with a sigh. "If she won't come . . ." I know Dr. Koios would help me, but he's so mild mannered. I feel as if I need a stronger god on my side.

"She will," Annie says. But I can see the doubt in her mind. "Listen, I'm sleeping over tonight. You don't have a say in the matter. Come on," she whispers, "let's clean this place up."

We start in the living room. I gently put the shards of glass in a brown paper trash bag from the grocery store, and Annie runs the vacuum cleaner. The two of us push the couch back up on its four legs. I pick up my mother's precious books that were scattered, and place them back on the coffee table. We put the desk drawers back into the desk and put all the papers and other items back where they belong.

Then we go to Mom's room and remake the bed and straighten up. I want her room to be perfect for if she comes back. For *when* she comes back. She *has* to come back.

When we're finished, I pull out my cell phone, thinking maybe I accidentally had it on silent and missed Aphrodite's call. But she hasn't called. I start to think she never will.

"Want to come to my house for dinner?" Annie asks. "You know my mom. Always enough for any extras at the table. I think tonight she was making meat loaf. You know how good hers is."

"No," I say, even as my mouth involuntarily waters at the thought of Mrs. Casey's home cooking. "It will be too hard to act as if everything is okay. I'm too much of a mess. Let's order sushi like we planned."

"How are you going to pay? Your grandpa's not here. And sushi isn't cheap."

I smile. "The cash drawer."

"The what?"

I lead her into the kitchen. Next to the take-out menu drawer is another drawer filled with cash. Grandpa always keeps a decent-size stash of just-in-case money around. There is usually at least a thousand dollars in it. Grandpa, before he retired, was a very successful architect with his own design firm and a bunch of employees.

He and my grandmother had a fancy house a few towns over in Piermont, on the water overlooking the Hudson—a house he designed with tall windows to take in the view. He always said he felt as if he was rattling around it once my grandmother died. Then, when my mom got sick, he sold it and moved in with us, even though our house is not as big and not as fancy. About the same time, he sold his design firm, too, for a lot of money.

He's always been determined to live life to the fullest since then, so we have amazing season tickets to the Yankees, right behind home plate. And we have a cash drawer where other people have spatulas and whisks.

"Holy crap!" Annie says. "How did I not know Grandpa kept a drawer of *cash*?"

I shrug. "I know, right?"

Annie calls her mom and tells her she's going to sleep over at my house. We sit down at the table with the Japanese menu to figure out our order when the doorbell rings.

I look warily at Annie. The last time I answered the door for delivery, things did not go well. I go to the pantry. On the bottom shelf is Grandpa's toolbox. I open it and pull out a hammer.

"Just in case," I whisper.

Annie and I creep to the front door, and I peer through the peephole. I open the door.

"Iris! Annie!" Aphrodite screams. "I came as soon as I got your call! Come to your aunt Aphrodite!" Then she pulls us to her, nearly crushing us both against her ample chest.

She enters the living room. Behind her is a *totally*

hot guy, head shaven and big muscles, in a tight-fitting black sweater and Levi's, carrying two huge suitcases plus a garment bag.

"This is Nico," she says. "This is my sweet, sweet niece, Iris, and her equally adorable best friend, Annie."

He puts down the suitcases. I put the hammer down on a bookshelf, and he shakes my hand. "Nice to meet you, Iris." He grins. When he smiles, he's even hotter, if that's possible. He's got this chasm of a dimple in his left cheek. Then he shakes Annie's hand. "Annie . . . nice to meet you." Her mouth is slightly agape.

He leans close to Aphrodite and kisses her neck. He whispers, sexily, "I'll go get the rest of your things out of the car."

"Thank you, Nico," she purrs.

When he goes outside, I ask, "Uh, is he staying here, too?"

"No, no. He wanted to, but . . . well, it would be best if he didn't know everything that's going on. He'll worry. I told him to stay with his bakery and that I'll check in."

Nico returns with *another* two suitcases. I don't want to stare, but I'm wondering how long Aphrodite thinks this is going to take—she's packed enough for a month. He makes one more trip and comes back with two large brown paper take-out bags.

"I hope you don't mind eating Greek tonight, girls," Aphrodite says. She removes the dramatic full-length opera cape she's wearing. Beneath it, she's wearing a black velvet dress, low cut and revealing cleavage, but perfectly hugging her hips. She is as blinged out as the first time we saw her, and if possible, her hair is teased even higher. And she's wearing a tiara. With what looks like real diamonds. I've decided Aphrodite is the *original* diva.

Nico walks through to the kitchen and puts the bags on the table. Then he comes back to kiss Aphrodite good-bye.

I almost have to look away. The kiss they share is so passionate. Like out of a movie or something.

He waves good-bye to the three of us and goes outside to his car—a black Mercedes SUV—and pulls away. He *had* to have an SUV just to fit all of Aphrodite's crap in it.

Aphrodite ushers us into the kitchen. She immediately starts opening cupboards, finding plates and cups. I move to help her, but she waves me away.

"No, no, you sit. You've been through a trauma."

Annie and I sit at the table. Aphrodite puts a plate

in front of each of us and one for herself at the head of the table. Then she starts unpacking the Greek takeout. There is souvlaki and meats wrapped in grape leaves. Other dishes emerge from containers, but I don't even know what they are. She pulls out pastries for dessert. I am suddenly reminded that I haven't eaten. My mouth waters spontaneously, despite how upset I am.

"Tell me everything," Aphrodite says when she has put all the food on the table. She opens a bottle of red wine for herself and hands Annie and me Cokes. Then she finally sits.

I tell her all about Dr. Koios, about the museum— again leaving out the part about Sebastian's hand under my T-shirt. I tell her about the bullets. I try to remember everything, every detail. I tell her about the conversation between Annie and me in the Volkswagen. I even tell her about our song. And then I tell her about coming home to the disaster. My mom. Grandpa. When I talk, my throat tightens, and I have to wipe at a stray tear with a napkin.

Aphrodite's face grows dark. I see, I swear, light flash in her eyes, like sparks. Her eyes are as blue as sapphires, but the sparks are real, like fireworks against a July summer sky. I am reminded she is a goddess, from another world.

"We'll get them back, I promise you. So help me Zeus," she says, and raises her right hand.

I exhale and look at Annie. I feel a little better with a goddess on my side.

"Give me the night to sleep on it. By tomorrow I'll have a plan. And don't worry. Epiales won't harm them, I don't think. He's doing this to scare you and to seriously piss off his brother. But for now, I'm sure they're safe. It's *you* he wants."

As if that makes me feel any better.

After dinner, I show Aphrodite to the guest room. She smiles. "This is quite lovely." She surveys the sleigh bed. It has one of my old mattresses on it—the pillow top that cost thousands and is supposed to be the most comfortable mattress ever made. It still never helped me sleep. "Just a few little changes," she murmurs.

She goes to the living room, where Nico left her suitcases. The garment bag is full of gowns and dresses. She brings it to her room and starts hanging things in the walk-in closet. I can't help but notice that all the gowns are designer fashions with expensive labels and extravagant fabrics. I didn't even know some of them made plus-size clothes.

The next suitcase is full of beauty supplies—creams that I know cost hundreds of dollars an ounce—and jewelry, all of which looks real. She also has hot rollers, curling irons, cans of hairspray, and framed pictures of Greece and one of Nico. She puts that one on the nightstand.

Back in the living room, she starts unpacking a suitcase filled with her beloved snow globes and other knickknacks. I smile to myself. My grandfather would have a fit. He's a believer in sleek design and simplicity. Every stick of furniture in our house he has handpicked. Even his reclining La-Z-Boy is leather and elegant-looking. She puts snow globes on the coffee table and on the bookshelves. Soon there's clutter everywhere.

After she's completely unpacked, she sits down. "Ah, this is so much better."

"We're going to go change into our pajamas. Annie is sleeping over, if that's okay." I need something to keep my mind off my missing family.

"Okay?" Her eyes sparkle like gemstones again. "I've never had a slumber party in all my thousands of years! How fun!"

While Annie and I change, so does Aphrodite. We come out in sweats and T-shirts. Aphrodite emerges from her bedroom in a negligee and robe, the collar of which is covered in real mink. She looks like a 1940s movie star. She is perched on heeled slippers with fur trim, and, of course, she's still wearing all her bling.

"All right. So what do we do at a slumber party?" She claps her hands excitedly. Her nails are perfectly manicured in an orchid color. There are rhinestones on the tips.

I'm still achy, but I have already come to adore my new aunt, and I don't want to disappoint her—especially since she has waited thousands of years for a sleepover.

"W-e-ll," I say, drawing out the word, "we usually make popcorn."

"And drink Red Bulls," adds Annie.

"Lots of them," I say. "Especially tonight, since Dr. Koios has warned me *not* to go down the hallway of my dreams."

"And we rent movies."

"Ooh, such fun!" Aphrodite croons.

"Only problem," I say, "is the only TV is in my room. The three of us will have to squeeze onto my bed."

"I wouldn't have it any other way. Do we get to talk about boys?"

"Of course," Annie and I say in unison.

We make the popcorn and raid the fridge for all the Red Bulls we have. I also remember we've got a large stash of Girl Scout cookies—Grandpa is a sucker for the little girl two doors down and always buys, like, a hundred dollars' worth—and a box of Raisinets. They are Grandpa's favorite candy. I take them out of the pantry, but then I feel my eyes water, so I put them back. I'll save them for when he is home safely. I grab a bag of Doritos instead.

The three of us squeeze into my bed. It's king-size anyway, so it's not too bad. We climb under the covers and pull them up and spread our feast over the quilt.

We let Aphrodite pick the movie. She opts for an old Hollywood musical, *Guys and Dolls*. Turns out she knows all the words to all the songs. And she sings along. Her voice is beautiful, like Celine Dion or Barbra Streisand.

We eat popcorn. And Thin Mints. And we laugh at the movie's funny parts. Aphrodite swoons over Marlon Brando. When the movie is over, I click on Jimmy Fallon, and we start talking boys.

"So Henry Wu and I had a moment," Annie says.

"I know."

"But you said we wouldn't get together until I was twenty-six."

"Nope. You're going to go to the Valentine's Day dance together, and you'll never be apart ever again.

You're going to go to Boston College so you can be near him while he's at Harvard."

Boston College is Annie's first choice of school, and she beams.

"But then my fortune wasn't true, what you said."

"Oh, it's *mostly* true. He will be the inventor of the next Facebook. He will fund your charity. But I knew if I told you the story the *first* way, you would be curious enough to give Henry a chance. Now your story will unfold the way it's really supposed to. Oh, and your first kiss? Henry is going to surprise you. That boy has had a *pent-up* love for you for so long, and all that passion is going to be in that kiss. I may move it up my list."

"Your list?" I ask.

"I keep a list of the top one hundred kisses of all time. They were at number thirty-one. But I might move them into the top twenty."

"Wow," Annie breathes out.

"In fact, Annie, like all couples, you'll face difficult times. Sadness. Loss. There's no escaping that for any of us. You will be mad at each other sometimes. But for both of you, the memory of that kiss will be so powerful, so strong, neither of you will *ever*, not for one second, consider leaving the other."

My throat constricts with happiness for Annie. I

squeeze her hand over Aphrodite, who is wedged between us.

I think of my kisses with Sebastian. The one in the club. I think it is the kind of kiss that could sustain me for a lifetime, too. If only a kiss like that could happen in the flesh. In my real world.

"So your turn, Aphrodite. You must have some amazing love affairs to talk about," I say.

"Well, you all know the one about Adonis and me, of course. Such a beautiful, beautiful man. But that was when I was . . . ahem . . . younger and more impetuous. I had a bit of a temper. I was the jealous type, too."

"What about Nico?" Annie asks.

"Oh, my." Aphrodite's cheeks turn red.

"All your lovers, and Nico makes you blush?" I ask incredulously. "But you've been with *gods*."

"When I came here to live among mortals," Aphrodite says, "I think I matured. I mean, if you can't learn something from centuries and centuries of existence . . . I am almost embarrassed by the stories and myths of me of old. Though don't believe every myth you hear, girls. Anyway, I came to see that there is something *incredibly* beautiful about a mortal man giving you his heart—openly. Nico has been hurt. He was married, briefly, in his early twenties. His wife was unfaithful to him with his own brother. He walked in on them in bed together three months after the wedding. They split up; she married the brother. Tore the family apart for quite some time."

Annie and I gasp.

"My God, but he's so hot," I say.

"His brother is, too. Maybe even hotter. But his brother has that bad-boy edge. Anyway, for a long time, Nico was a very wounded person. He carried this pain tucked in his heart, a scar. And every time he even thought about letting himself love again, that scar would throb—it would ache and remind him of how much he had been hurt."

"And?" Annie snuggles down, her head on her pillow, hanging on to Aphrodite's every word.

"And he met me." She beams. "And little by little, he shared his heart, until he gave all of it, totally, to me. And I know what an act of courage that was. And it might be the most beautiful, most precious gift a man or god has ever given me. I have had my naked body draped in diamonds and rubies and pearls. I have had men worship me. But Nico is different. He has a pure heart. Not to mention, we're number one."

I raise an eyebrow at her, questioningly.

"The hottest kiss," she squeals, and the three of us laugh.

I yawn.

Aphrodite looks concerned.

"If I see you having a nightmare, I'm waking you up," she says. "These Red Bulls? I just may be awake all night."

"I'll be okay," I whisper. "If I come to the hallway, I'll turn back. I promise."

"Just the same, I'm going to stay up awhile. You two girls go to sleep." She glances over at Annie, who is already exhaling the heavy breaths of sleep.

My eyelids flutter. I feel Aphrodite gently stroking my hair.

"Hush, Iris. Go to sleep. Your aunt Aphrodite will protect you tonight."

I realize how the exhaustion and emotional upset have caught up with me. And finally, I succumb to the blackness.

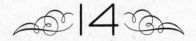

14

Man is a genius when he is dreaming.
AKIRA KUROSAWA

My eyes flutter. I wake up. Aphrodite is next to me, asleep. Even in slumber, I notice how exquisite she is—whereas Annie tells me when I sleep I sometimes snore and occasionally drool. Aphrodite's lips form a perfect bow, her eyebrows are an elegant arch. Her skin is flawless. I realize now that she's ageless. I can't tell whether in her mortal form she's twenty-five or thirty-five or forty. She has not one wrinkle. And yet, her confidence is the confidence of a woman with wisdom.

Annie yawns and stretches. Then she realizes Aphrodite is right next to her, and she tries to be quiet and move as little as possible.

But Aphrodite's eyes pop open. They are as glittery

and alive as sapphires under light. I guess she never really tires.

"Good morning, my angels." She reaches out her arms and gives each of us a squeeze. Then she furrows her brow. "Did you sleep?"

"Yeah," I say. "But I didn't dream. Not that I remember anyway."

The three of us get up. Annie and I wash and brush our teeth and get dressed. Annie raids my closet and picks jeans and a sweater in a soft gray that looks great against her skin. I pick a pair of black jeans and a vintage T-shirt. I put a black cardigan on, and we make our way to the kitchen.

I start a pot of coffee. "Want eggs?" I ask Annie. Usually, we would just have cereal or Pop-Tarts, but I feel as if a goddess probably wants eggs and bacon and a whole spread.

"Sure," Annie says.

I take out the skillet and start cooking breakfast. When it's just about done, Aphrodite emerges in a strapless bustier and dressy black pants, perched on rhinestone-encrusted Louboutins, by the looks of them.

"I'm famished," she announces. She takes orange juice from the fridge, pours us all glasses, and makes toast. Then I bring the eggs and bacon to the table and we start eating.

"I've decided how it is we're going to get back your mother and grandfather."

"How?" I ask.

"I don't know why I didn't think of it before. You're going to ask your father for help."

I practically choke on my piece of bacon, and Annie spews a little of her orange juice.

"Aphrodite," I say when I recover after a couple of coughs, "I've never met him. I mean, just a couple of times—snatches, when I didn't even know he was my father. And what am I going to do?" I pull my cell phone out of my back pocket. "Call him? In the Underworld, the dreamworld? 'Hey, Dad, even though you've never been a part of my life, and you're a god and all, I need a favor.' And I—I mean, if he's warring with Epiales, then he hardly has time to fix this problem for me."

"Trust me. He'll come."

"Still, how can I reach him?"

"We're going to have Koios come here, hypnotize you, and tell you how to get in touch with him. Morpheus may already know about your mother, but if he doesn't, I can promise you, there will be hell to pay. The Underworld will have a full-scale war on its hands. And that will mean Hades and Zeus will have no choice but to intervene to keep the balances of power in effect, and force Epiales to behave himself." She snaps her fingers. "Problem solved. One, two, three."

Annie looks at me anxiously. "Sounds risky. And not so simple."

"We have no choice, Annie," Aphrodite says softly. "I love both you girls. I don't want anything bad to happen. But I have no idea where Epiales may have taken Iris's mother and grandfather. It could be the Underworld; he could be hiding them in this realm. And until he gets what he wants, they are in danger—and if not real danger then certainly they are beside themselves with worry. And Iris surely isn't safe. And neither are you."

"Me?" Annie asks.

"Yes. You and her grandfather and mother are the three people Iris loves more than anything in the whole world. And there is nothing more powerful than that—and Epiales knows it."

Aphrodite's phone rings—her ringtone is Nelly Furtado's "Maneater."

"Hello?" she answers in a singsong voice.

"Yes, Nico, I'm fine. . . . Yes, they are lovely girls. Excellent students . . . Yes, I'm not sure yet when her mother and grandfather will be back. Visiting a sick relative, touch and go. But as soon as they do, I'll be back in Queens in your arms where I belong. . . . No, you cannot stay here. Yes, of course I miss you. No, no visiting. Just too much going on . . . Yes, I know how much you miss me." She lowers her voice. "But just *think* of how hot it will be when we are finally reunited."

I exchange glances with Annie, slight smirks on both our faces. To give Aphrodite a little privacy, we begin to clean up from breakfast. I wash the skillet, and Annie loads the dishwasher. We can hear Aphrodite whispering sweet nothings to Nico.

She and Nico finish their call, and the three of us take our cups of coffee into the living room. I forgot about the snow globes and knickknacks, so when I see all the chaos on the coffee table and bookcases, I laugh to myself for a second.

Aphrodite makes a phone call.

"Koi? It's me. Aphrodite."

She explains the situation. When she hangs up, she says he'll be here in about thirty minutes. We drink our coffee and read the paper, and Aphrodite gives herself a manicure, now painting her nails a scarlet color and putting a tiny rhinestone on each of her pinkies. She's blowing on her nails to dry them when Dr. Koios arrives.

I let him in, and he gives Annie and me hugs, then kisses Aphrodite on each cheek. He blushes a light pink when he does so. I think he has a little crush on her.

He decides I should sit in Grandpa's La-Z-Boy and recline it so I can relax into my hypnosis. Aphrodite stands and comes over and kisses me on my forehead.

"Remember you are powerful. You are *my* niece. And I love you. Come back to us when Koi tells you to, no matter what is going on in the dreamworld."

"I know."

"Promise me."

I don't like to break promises—ever. I think about it. Could I leave my mom or Grandpa, or Sebastian, if any of them were in trouble and Dr. Koios was calling me?

"I promise." I hope I can keep my vow.

Aphrodite and Annie sit on the couch. Dr. Koios pulls the desk chair over so he is right next to me.

"You know the drill, Iris," he says. This time he takes my left hand and squeezes it. "We're all here for you."

"How will I find my father?"

"The same way you found Sebastian last time. Trust yourself."

I exhale and shut my eyes. His soothing voice goes through the same routine.

"Relax into the chair. As you enter the deepest part of your hypnotic state, go down the hallway of many doors."

I am in the long, dark hallway, only this time I have the sconces to guide me. I walk down, pausing at each set of doors to look left and right, staring at each door, hoping one will feel like the portal that will take me to Morpheus.

I come to a door painted with clouds. It feels as infinite as the sky, but it does not speak to me in my gut. I hesitate but move on.

The hallway never ends. When I have walked what feels like a mile, I stop. Behind me are the hundreds of doors that I have passed. In front of me are the hundreds of doors still to come. This is not working. I do not feel my father, maybe because I have never really had one. I don't know what it is like. Morpheus is no more my father than the beautiful man in the painting with Iris. He is oil on canvas. I have no connection to him except birthright.

The one being I have a connection to in this strange world of dreams is Sebastian. I decide to find him, and together we will seek Morpheus. This is my new plan, and I have to go with it.

I shut my eyes. I think of kissing Sebastian. I

remember the time he lifted my hair in the hot nightclub and blew on my neck. My spine feels tingly.

I open my eyes and look at the doors. The door with swans on it isn't here. I walk on. I pass a black door engraved with some sort of Chinese or Asian symbol. I pass one painted royal purple, fit for a king. Then a door with intricate latticework. Finally, after walking for a while, I reach one that is simple wide-planked pine, with a heart-shaped red porcelain knob. I pause. My belly trembles. I touch the door. It quivers ever so slightly, like touching my phone when it's on vibrate.

This is it. I exhale. Sebastian must be my true one, because I feel him in a way that goes beyond words.

I fumble with the key ring until I find a key with a heart engraved on it. It is warm against my fingers. I insert it into the lock and hear the click. I inhale and open the door.

This room is very cold. And very dark. And I hear noises around me. A cacophony of frogs and nocturnal woodland creatures, like owls. I can't see anything.

"Remember this is your dream, Iris. You always have the tools you need." Dr. Koios's voice seems to whisper in my head.

I look down at my hands. The key ring has been replaced by a lantern. I lift it and shine the light all around me.

I am in the woods. Copses of long-needled pine trees surround me, and when I inhale, the scent is pine and that fresh tang of the winter when it's about to snow. My breath curls out from my mouth and around my face, and I shiver. My nose runs a little.

I look down at my sneakers, and I can see the ground is thick with a cushion of pine needles. But when I walk, the ground crunches beneath me, thick with frost.

I walk forward because I feel as if that's my only choice, but there's no discernible path. I gaze up through a break in the trees. A full moon peeks through slate-colored clouds, offering me just a little more light.

Still, I'm uneasy. I'm afraid of the dark. I always have been. Why here? Why this room? This forest?

I continue my steps, teeth chattering. Why is it so cold? I wish I had gloves. And a coat. They don't materialize. So I feel each gust of wind blowing past me.

From some far-off place, the mournful howl of a wolf pierces the night. The sound rips through me like a razor. Other wolves echo in return.

I don't like this. Everything about this room seems

wrong. But the Underworld, this netherworld, doesn't always make sense.

Sebastian, where are you?

I look behind me, and I no longer see the door.

Trust your power. Trust your instincts.

I calm myself. Inhale. Exhale. Just like Dr. Koios has taught me. Part of me wants to run. To go back, to find myself safe in my living room with Annie and Aunt Aphrodite and Dr. Koios. My shivering from the cold seems only to compound my unease and fright. But I know until this thing with Epiales is settled, I will never be safe, and neither will anyone I love.

I concentrate on my connection to Sebastian. When I think about him, instead of feeling my fear, I somehow know he is in this forest . . . somewhere. But I don't know why I cannot hear him calling to me. I miss his voice in my head. I feel lonely without him guiding me. I realize now that I have heard him in my head, almost like my conscience, for a long, long time. Now that I don't feel him . . . I miss it, that voice. I miss him.

I march on, holding my lantern in front of me. I hear some kind of animal padding on the forest floor, crunching its paws against the frost. I pray it's not a bear. I try to swallow, but my mouth is dry with fear.

Then, in the distance, I see it. A grin flits across my lips.

A log cabin perched on a small rise. And a sliver of light streams out from a crack in one of the windows, though its shades are drawn.

Of course. A romantic cabin in the woods where we can talk freely, no one finding us in this thick forest. Sebastian is brilliant.

I begin running toward it. The creature behind me growls, a rich-throated rumble that I feel in the core of my gut. I run faster, even though I'm pretty sure that if you encounter a bear, you're supposed to hold very still.

The creature must be large, because branches are breaking, their cracking sounds echoing through the dark night. My lungs burn as I run. My heart beats like a jackhammer in my ears. I've never been like Annie. I get winded climbing two flights of stairs.

The cabin is closer.

My legs ache and feel like lead, and I don't dare turn around.

Jaws snap behind me just as I reach the cabin porch.

I inhale sharply, hoping the door is unlocked. But it is my dream, and I turn the knob and the door swings open. I jump inside, slamming the door on *what is most definitely an enraged black bear that roars its disapproval, angrily slamming its body against the door, jolting me.*

I lock the door and turn around, heaving and sucking for air.

And then I see this dream is very, very wrong. It is very, very evil. Aphrodite is right. I could never have given voice to this. It is a nightmare, and I want to wake up—but don't dare.

Sebastian is tied to a wooden chair, heavy rope binding his wrists and each ankle secured to a leg of the chair. The light I had seen shining out is actually the light of an interrogation lamp hanging from the ceiling, a bare bulb, its beams so bright tears well involuntarily in my eyes. I blink hard and put my hand up as a shield.

I see a man dressed in black, like a Navy SEAL or some kind of assassin, standing next to Sebastian. The man's face is as brutal and hard-set as Epiales. He has black strips painted under his eyes and green-gray camouflage paint on his skin. Strapped to his waist is a sheath for a large knife. His eyes are those of a lizard, black and shiny and without feeling. Not quite human. Or maybe a sociopath. He is twice my size.

I clap my hand over my mouth to stop myself from screaming. Sebastian is bloody. He has been beaten. Severely. His face is barely recognizable, it is so battered and red and swollen. His head is drooped toward his chest. His lips are swollen, too. His hair is matted against his forehead. Blood drips from one corner of his mouth. One arm looks misshapen and broken in the restraints, or perhaps his shoulder is dislocated. His shirt is drenched with the sweat of a tortured and brutalized man, mixed with his own blood.

Aphrodite is right. Why do some people think this sort of scene is entertainment? It is not a movie. This is what suffering really is, what it really looks like and smells like. I can smell pain in the small cabin. I cannot imagine what he has been through.

I think he's dead, and I collapse to my knees. Now that I've found him, it cannot end this way. This cannot be.

"Iris . . . are you okay? I think you may need to come back. You aren't breathing normally. Own your power, Iris. Regain control."

But then Sebastian's chest rises.

I exhale in relief. He's alive. And if he's alive, then he can be healed.

The torturer smiles. A smile that sends such a frozen jolt up my spine, I literally shudder. My body fights against itself, in an internal war. Every nerve ending is screaming at my brain, "Run!" Save myself. Wake myself up.

And my heart and soul are rooted to the floor of that cabin. I will not abandon him.

"He wouldn't call for you."

"What?" I whisper, shocked I can even make a sound. I have no idea what this evil man means.

"All he had to do was call for you. Like he always has. Bring you here. But he wouldn't. And this"—he sweeps his hand at Sebastian's destroyed face as if he is showing off a work of art on display—"is the result. Doesn't appear as good-looking as the last time you saw him, does he? Pity. Does he still make your heart flutter?"

No, I think, he makes my heart hurt for his pain.

"Iris?" Sebastian lifts his head slightly.

His voice is so broken. I don't care about the man in black. I pull myself to my feet and run to Sebastian, kneeling down by his side and placing my head in his lap. I feel and smell his blood, warm and coppery and slightly sticky, on my cheek and seeping into my hair. I place my hand on his chest, stroke his belly, afraid my very touch will hurt him more.

"Let him go," I say, looking up at the man.

He just laughs at me.

"Please." I hate the begging tone in my voice. "I don't know what you want."

"You're right. You don't. You're just a pawn in a bigger plan."

I'm confused. There is clearly something more than just jealousy at work in the Underworld. I know it now. Just hating my humanity would be too simple. The treachery and intrigue between the gods knows no bounds. They have raped one another, gouged out eyes, deceived, kidnapped, committed adultery, destroyed one another. But right now I am too terrified to figure out Epiales's bigger plan. I just want to get Sebastian and me out of here alive.

"When my father finds out what you've done, there will be no place in the Underworld to keep you safe."

The man sneers. Then he makes a fist and punches Sebastian as hard as he can—he does it so fast, Sebastian can't even brace for it. His neck snaps back. I hear bone crunching in Sebastian's cheek.

I scream and stand, blocking Sebastian's body with my own. I brace myself for a blow, and he delivers a brutal open-palmed slap across my face. My eyes blur with tears, and my nose starts to run. In the corner of my mouth, I taste my own sweet-salty blood.

"Iris, no!" Sebastian begs me. But I don't cower. I tilt my head up to say this man cannot defeat me. This is my power. Daughter of Morpheus. My power is I see my great and unspoken fear in front of me, that which I could have never given voice to, but I am willing to suffer for those I love.

The man steps toward me, and I think he's going to hit me again. Instead, he pulls a jagged knife from the sheath on his belt. The blade is huge, and it gleams in the bright light. I try to swallow but find I can't.

Staring at me impassively, he drops the knife on the wooden floor with a thud.

"Cut him free," he says. "I'm done here."

Then the man walks to the door of the cabin and opens it. The bear is gone.

"It's been fun." He leers.

With that, he walks out of the cabin and into the darkness beyond, slamming the door behind him.

Frantically, I cut the ropes, and Sebastian screams in agony as blood rushes into his injured arm and numb hands.

I want to vomit. I have loved my mother through her long illness, but it is a clean illness. She's asleep. I was a baby when my grandmother died. I know the cancer was brutal to her, shriveling her once-vibrant body to a mere ninety pounds. But I have never seen someone I love suffer. Not like this. My admiration for Grandpa grows even more. I know being my grandmother's caretaker was incredibly difficult.

"Can you walk?" I whisper.

"I can try."

I stand on his other side, away from his injured arm. I slide my shoulder under his arm and try to pull him to his feet. He staggers and collapses back into the chair.

I look around the cabin and see cupboards and a sink.

You are in control of your dream, Iris, I remind myself, though I don't feel like the master of my own dream.

I race to the cabinets and open them. They are all empty. I shut one of the cabinet doors and gather my thoughts. Control this. When I open it again, I find a first-aid kit. I also take off my sweater and T-shirt, stripping down to my bra. I put the sweater back on and soak my soft tee in water to clean his wounds.

Back at his side, I press the wet T-shirt against his face, dabbing away at the caked-on blood. He winces.

"I'm sorry," I whisper.

One eye is swollen shut, but he looks at me with his other eye. "You look beautiful tonight, Iris."

I shake my head. "And . . . I can't say the same for you."

He offers me a feeble laugh, and I lean up to kiss his lips, as gently as possible.

"I wouldn't call for you. I didn't want you to come here, Iris."

"I felt you."

"I felt you as soon as you came in the door from the dream hallway. I ached for you."

My stomach does the flip-flop I always feel when I hear him talk or see him.

"I don't know how much time we have," I whisper hurriedly. "Where there's one of those evil souls, there are many, and now they know where we are. We need to go, Sebastian. Help me. How do I find my father? I need to speak with him. He has to know my mother and grandfather have been taken."

"Taken?"

I nod. "Violently. In my world. By Epiales or his men."

Sebastian's lone good eye flashes like lightning. "I will bring a message to him. They will pay for this."

"You're in no condition to go."

"I'm immortal. My wounds will heal quickly. I felt every blow. I didn't suffer any less. But I will heal. Soon."

Even as he says this, I see bruises receding. I touch

his cheekbone softly. "Amazing," I whisper.

I keep dressing his wounds and cleaning him up. Eventually, he feels well enough to stand.

"We've got to get out of here," he says.

"Let's go."

We walk to the cabin door and step out onto the porch. The forest looks no less uninviting. I don't want to go into its darkness, which has grown eerier. A fog has settled near the ground. The moon is shrouded.

He takes my hand with his good arm, and we start out the way I came. Again I hear the wolves howling. But the bear is nowhere in sight.

We walk deeper into the forest's depths. Branches slap my face. A soft, freezing drizzle starts.

"Great," I mutter. "Just what we need." The icy rain pelts my arms and face, stinging me.

And then I hear growling, rumbles. I look at one of the pine trees and see pairs of eyes glowing yellow in the underbrush.

I stop. I hear panting.

"Sebastian," I whisper, "it's a wolf pack."

The beasts snarl, baring their teeth. One emerges from the underbrush. I assume it's the alpha male. It snaps its teeth and lowers its head, and the black fur on its back stands on end. The wolf's tail is lowered. The rumble is deep in its chest.

"On three, we run," Sebastian whispers.

"Where?"

"To the door."

But I know the door disappeared as soon as I walked into this nightmare. I will have to do what I did at the museum. And after the trauma of this night, I don't feel confident that I can.

But there's no time to discuss it.

"One . . . two . . . three," he says.

The two of us break into a run. He grunts in pain beside me.

It's time for me to let my instincts take over. I stop thinking and just move.

The beasts snap at our heels. I hear them, their snarls and snapping jaws.

"Turn left," I scream, trusting my gut, trying to think but then just reacting. There is no time to think. The wolves are too close.

We race to the left. I feel blood on my face, sharp branches blinding me to what little I can see in the darkness, scratching me.

"Iris, you *must* come back now. Immediately." Dr. Koios's voice is insistent.

"Please," Aphrodite says. "Or you're grounded!"

A wolf is at my side, its fur brushing against the back of my hand. It bites at my leg. My pants rip open, and its teeth puncture my calf.

I can make out a clearing ahead, and when we get there, the wolves surround us. I know I made a promise to Dr. Koios, but I can't leave Sebastian. Not hurt. Not to face them alone.

Sebastian stops, pulling me to him. "Go!" he urges me.

And there, carved in an immense tree, as wide and thick as a redwood, is a door.

"Go through it with me!" I say as he tugs me to the door.

"Not until Epiales is defeated. I need to get your message to your father."

I start to argue with him, but instead he kisses my mouth, hard and hungry. Then he opens the door and pushes me through it, even as I hear him roar in pain as the first wolf attacks.

I hurt so much, at first I can't move. Even my eyelashes hurt.

Dr. Koios says, "Open your eyes, Iris."

I do. I'm in my home, in my grandfather's chair. And the reality that I didn't find Morpheus, that I am no closer to bringing back my mother and grandfather, sits on my chest like a heavy stone.

"I wasn't sure you would come back," Annie says. "I'll go get you some water."

She goes to the kitchen and comes back with a Diet Coke instead. She pops the tab and hands it to me. When I lift my hand to take it, I see bruising on the back of my hand. I sip the soda and then touch my face. It's puffy. But unlike Sebastian, I don't heal quickly. It's getting harder and harder to cover my misadventures in the dreamworld with makeup.

"I'm freezing," I whisper. "Can you get me a blanket?"

Annie runs to fetch one. She returns and covers me with a soft quilt. I still shake from a chill. I'm so cold I wonder if I will ever feel warm again.

Aphrodite is trembling. "She wasn't the only one worried you weren't coming back. Now that you have found me, I can't lose you, Iris. Don't ever do that again. You can't. I forbid it."

"I wouldn't have come back if Sebastian hadn't pushed me through. . . . I didn't find Morpheus." Tears press against my eyes. I picture Sebastian being mauled by the wolves. I remember the pain of just a single blow from the man in black and feel anguished by the thought of what happened in that cabin before I got there.

"And Aunt Aphrodite, you were right. Epiales tormented me with something that will scar me forever."

I shut my eyes. But the images of today are seared into the memory of my soul mate suffering for me.

15

*Between living and dreaming
there is a third thing. Guess it.*
ANTONIO MACHADO

Annie helps me up. Limping, I go to take a hot shower. I stay in there until the water runs tepid, and I finally start to warm up, my fingers no longer icicles. When I step out, after the mist clears, I look at the bruises in the mirror. A short time ago, I was insomniac girl. An ordinary girl with an ordinary problem.

And now I am someone different. A demi-goddess with a very, very big problem.

I dab on some cover-up, hoping, somehow, it will make Aphrodite worry a little less. I change into yoga pants and a tank top, and put my softest, most comfortable cardigan on over it. Before I go out to

Annie and the others, I walk into Grandpa's bedroom. He has a king-size bed with yet another of my failed mattresses on it. The room is him—his computer is perched on an architect's drawing table. On the wall are framed prints of buildings he admires, like the Chrysler in Manhattan. He has a couple of framed autographs of Yankees players, including a Roger Maris. The room smells of Grandpa's cologne. I slide open his closet doors and touch his neatly pressed shirts—he always sends them to the dry cleaner; aside from not being able to cook, laundry isn't his thing, either. I miss him so much I feel as if I can barely stand.

When I come back into the living room, I tell them everything that happened in the Underworld. Including the line that I was a "pawn."

Aphrodite and Dr. Koios exchange looks. "Hmm," he says. He taps his index fingers together like he does when he's thinking. "That's very interesting."

"I know," I say. "All this time, I thought Epiales just hated me for my existence. But now I think it's something more."

Aphrodite bites one corner of her mouth. Her eyes do that fireworks thing again.

The doorbell rings. We all jump.

"Think we're a little freaked out?" Annie jokes.

"I'll answer it," Dr. Koios says. He grabs the fireplace tongs. Just in case.

But when he opens the door, it is not Epiales or one of his menacing sidekicks.

There, standing on the doorstep, is my father.

"Morpheus," I exhale.

Dr. Koios ushers him in. My father stares straight at me, as if no one else is in the room. He looks just like the painting, with thick locks of curly hair and an ageless, porcelain face like Aphrodite's. I stare back at him, looking to see what features he has that are like my own. I have his nose, and I guess his curls. I think I may have his cheekbones, too. But I have my mother's mouth, and the curve of her neck.

"Iris . . ." His voice is husky.

I don't want to cry. I don't even know, for sure, what to feel. I always had Grandpa, but there were times when I was at Annie's house when I would see the way her dad was with her. It was usually something simple, like the times he'd come upstairs to her room, admonish us with "Don't tell Mom," and hand us these amazing ice-cream-sundae creations. Or when stupid Mike O'Malley broke Annie's heart, and he just sat with her and me, and let her cry. Those times, I longed for a father.

I used to imagine that there was something

complicated to my birth. That my father wasn't a sperm donor and that someday he would come looking for me. But right now, I'm just a jumble.

Aunt Aphrodite is standing next to him. "Come here, Iris," she says.

I stand and walk to her, feeling numb, and she envelops me in a hug. Not one of her boob-crushing, over-the-top hugs, but a mom hug, as if sheltering me like a baby bird under a wing.

"It's okay," she whispers in my ear. "He's your father, and he loves you."

She releases me and tucks a stray curl behind my ear. Morpheus steps to me and hesitates, but then he puts his arms around me. I lean my head against his chest. All the years of being a fatherless girl melt away. It is like the times I would watch Mr. Casey hug Annie after a soccer match, and I would think that there was a spot—right there—just so, for her head to rest. This is what it feels like.

We stand there for a few minutes, and then he pulls away.

"Tell me about your mother and grandfather." His voice is stronger and deeper than I thought it would be. But it is reassuring.

"Did Sebastian tell you?"

He nods.

My throat constricts.

So I tell him everything, about coming home to the mess and Mom being gone. At the word *gone*, I choke up so badly I can't speak. He takes both my hands and holds them in his, which are strong.

"I stayed away for so many years, wanting to spare you from the treachery of the Underworld. It can be a dangerous place, and my brothers and the Keres are among the most dangerous of all. I never wanted to draw attention to you or your mother."

"But she's been visiting you in her sleep all these years."

"I unfairly drew her to me. I couldn't bear eternity without her. But as my child, I thought it was best to ensure you remained in this mortal world. Believe me, Iris. You must believe, my child, that if I could have been here with you, I would have been. Your safety was my number-one concern. Your happiness—and hers—are all I care about."

"So get her back," I whisper.

"I don't know where he's taken her, and the Underworld is falling into a state of anarchy. Epiales is amassing armies . . . and allies."

"I don't understand what he wants."

"Neither do I."

"So what do we do?" I ask.

He smiles. He lifts my hands to his cheek. Then he kisses the backs of my hands. "My precious, precious baby girl, *we* do not do anything. You leave this to me. I *will* get your mother back."

I want to believe him. But I have seen what Epiales can do. I hate thinking of what he might be doing to my mother and Grandpa. Maybe Sebastian. Right now.

"Is Sebastian all right?" I ask him. "He . . . pushed me through the door from your world to this one, and I know they attacked him."

Morpheus's face grows impassive.

"What?" I ask.

"Sebastian is missing. Unaccounted for."

"What?" I can't swallow. The room feels hot. It seems like just a short while ago I thought I'd freeze.

"I'll find him. Don't worry."

Dr. Koios says, "Is Hades aware of all that is occurring?"

"I plan to go see him."

"You haven't gone to him yet?" Aphrodite says. "My god, I have him and Zeus on my speed dial."

"Really?" Annie asks.

"Of course not." Aphrodite laughs lightly. "Come on. Let's sit down and eat. Pastries help me think better."

Food may help Aphrodite, but I know I can't eat.

The five of us stand and start toward the kitchen. I can't believe I'm going to sit and share a table with my father. It feels more like a dream than reality. But I pinch the top of my hand, and I know this is real. Though maybe I don't know anything about what's truly real anymore. Now if only the rest of my family—and Sebastian—were here.

They are all ahead of me when I feel the most sickening pain my stomach, a pain like I've never felt before. It's a sharp stabbing, like being gutted by a knife, followed by a burning throb. It's agony. I double over, and all the blood drains from my face.

I can't help it—I groan involuntarily.

Annie wheels around. She runs and kneels in front of me. "My God, Iris, what is it?"

I can't speak. I can't breathe. I clutch my stomach and moan, tears streaming down my face, and I don't even care who sees me cry.

"Annie," I manage to breathe out. "Help me." It has to be my appendix. Bursting. I hurt so bad, I think I want to die. That anything would be preferable to this pain.

Aphrodite shrieks. "I don't know how to drive. Koi, bring your car around—we'll take her to the hospital."

She comes over to me and puts her hand on my forehead. "She's burning up. My god . . . Morpheus." She looks to my father. His face is disbelieving, and he comes to me and literally lifts me and holds me in his arms like a small child.

I can't understand how I got so sick so fast. Something is really wrong with me. I try to talk. But the pain is so bad, I feel myself passing out, my vision narrowing to two tiny pinpoints.

The last words I hear are "Forget the car, Koi. Call nine-one-one."

And then nothing.

Dreams are stories made by and for the dreamer, and each dreamer has his own folds to open and knots to untie.

SIRI HUSTVEDT

I wake in a white-sheeted hospital bed, my hair matted against an uncomfortable pillow. The pain has been replaced by a drug-induced haze. But despite pain medication, my stomach is still throbbing its discomfort, occasionally a real spasm of torturous agony. I can tell by my drenched sheets that the fever remains.

Morpheus and Aunt Aphrodite are here. For the first time, Aphrodite looks a mess. Her eyes are swollen from crying. She's knotting a tissue in her hands. I try to look around, but everything is foggy, like seeing through a mist. I lift my left hand and see an IV taped in place. Machines are beeping. Plastic bags of medicine and fluids hang from poles around me, like silent sentinels, a half-dozen things being pumped into me.

"What's wrong with me?" I ask. My voice is raspy. I want my toothbrush.

Aphrodite starts weeping softly. "The doctors aren't sure. They're bringing in a couple of specialists tonight. They're running tests."

A doctor and a nurse walk in. The doctor is wheeling a gunmetal gray cart with a laptop on it. She says hello to me, a thin blond woman with a sleek, professional bob and pale-green-rimmed glasses.

"Hi," I whisper.

"You gave us quite a fright last night, Iris."

"Do you know anything yet, Doctor?" my father asks.

"Her results are very . . . confusing. Her white counts are as high as numbers we would see in someone with leukemia, but other blood results that I would expect to be elevated aren't, and those I would expect to be low are high. In other words, your daughter is very sick, but we don't know, right now, from what. Her spleen is very enlarged. I'm a bit concerned that we might need to remove it surgically."

"And my appendix?" I ask.

"Fine. Sometimes we can't see it clearly on an

ultrasound, but we were lucky with you. Perfectly healthy. As is your gallbladder. So those're two things ruled out for right now. A spot of good news in all this. I've asked your parents here if you've traveled overseas recently."

I realize she thinks Aphrodite is my mother. I shake my head weakly. I don't think the Underworld counts as overseas.

"We've checked with your school—closed for the holidays, but the superintendent called back. No infectious disease outbreaks. No exposures to heavy metals. Apparently"—she smiles—"you eat a lot of takeout."

I nod, wondering what that has to do with this.

"We've checked all those restaurants. No hepatitis outbreaks. Nothing. And the suddenness. That's quite concerning. You are very much a mystery, which I am sure you don't want to hear with a one-hundred-four-degree fever that I'm positive is making you feel awful. We haven't been able to get that down. Last night you spiked one hundred five point two."

My teeth chatter from my fever. As if I didn't already know, I am realizing how very sick I am.

"We've started a strong antibiotic, an antinausea medicine, and we're treating your pain with morphine and Dilaudid. That's another reason you feel so woozy and out of it. Because of that, if you have to get up to use the bathroom, you need to call for your nurse. We don't want you to fall."

The doctor comes over to my bedside. "Mind if I give a listen?"

"Sure."

She presses a stethoscope to my belly and then my chest. She asks me to sit up. I try, and it sends shooting pains through my abdomen and up my spine to the base of my skull. I cry out.

"Don't!" Aphrodite exclaims. "I can't stand to see her suffer like this. Let her rest."

The doctor smiles compassionately at my aunt. "I'll try to keep her as comfortable as possible. I know this is very upsetting."

My heart is pounding. The nurse, a strawberry-blonde with freckles, takes my blood pressure.

"It's one ninety-five over one forty."

Looking at the nurse, my doctor, whose badge reads B. BINGHAM, M.D., says, "Gladys, I think we're going to change her pain meds around, see if we can't get better pain control. I'm sure the pain and fever are elevating her blood pressure. Give her the pain medication every three hours now instead of four.

We may end up putting her on a pump."

The doctor walks to the laptop and punches some keys. She pushes her glasses down to the end of her nose and appears to be studying something on the screen.

"We'll be drawing some more blood later. We're like vampires around here." She smiles, but all I can think of are the Keres. How anyone can think vampires are sexy is beyond me.

The doctor and the nurse leave. Morpheus's face is intense. Like Aphrodite, his eyes flash alive. I swear I see lightning. Clouds gather on the surface of his irises. They are mesmerizing.

"I don't think these doctors will be able to help you," Morpheus says.

"Why?"

"If Sebastian is missing, I can think of only one thing to torment him with."

He looks down at me. "You."

I feel as if I'm going to die.

The nurse comes back in holding a syringe. "I have your pain medication here."

Morpheus blinks, and his eyes return to normal.

"We're going to go into the hallway to talk," Aphrodite murmurs. "Annie is here in the visitors' lounge. I'll send her in for a few minutes, but not too long, sweetie. You need your rest. Nico will be driving up to Nyack later. There was no keeping him away, given this crisis. He refuses to listen to reason."

I smile weakly. Nico seems like a really good guy, and I love Aphrodite so much, it's what she deserves.

Aphrodite points to my IV bag. "For now, *that's* the only 'food' you're getting. You can't have anything to eat or drink until they figure out what's wrong with your stomach, but once you can, Nico will bring us every pastry he makes, my darling."

The nurse says softly, "This is your pain medication." She inserts the syringe into my IV. I feel a warmth and then a huge woozy rush. I see double and then feel as if I'm floating on air. I feel kind of happy. And kind of nauseous. And kind of stupid. I can't think. My father kisses me.

"I love you, Iris," he whispers.

"I love you, too . . . Morpheus." I can't bring myself to use the D-word yet. But it's progress.

Aphrodite kisses me. She strokes my hair. "Your father will watch over you tonight, right in that chair. I'm going to go home to shower and change. When I come back, I'll bring a brush and pretty pajamas and your toothbrush . . . and your iPod. And phone. And chargers. Anything else?"

"Feed Puck."

"The cat?"

I nod. "His food is"—my voice drifts off as I slip into a doze. When my head bobs to the side, it wakes me up, and I add—"under the sink in the kitchen."

They leave. My father looks back and says, "I'll be right outside your door."

Annie comes in—with Henry Wu. I can't believe I'm letting him see me like this. My hair on a *good* day after sleeping on it looks like a fright wig. But I'm so medicated I kind of don't care how he sees me. Besides, he's so gaga for Annie, I don't know that he even cares.

She leans down to kiss me. "You scared the crap out of me. You seem to be doing a lot of that lately."

"Sorry." The medication makes me feel as if I can't talk, but at least the throbbing in my belly is a little better, this tiny bit of relief.

"Sorry you're so sick, Iris," Henry whispers. He looks concerned. I also notice he's holding Annie's hand.

"Something you two want to tell me?" I mumble.

They exchange looks. Annie flushes. "I texted him that you were sick. And he came right to the hospital instead of answering me."

"How long have I been here?"

"A whole night. And it's almost five o'clock, Monday."

"What?" I hear the panic in my own voice. I try to sit up, but agony sets in again.

"Lie there, Iris. I'm ordering you."

"You should rest," Henry says. He looks awkward, like he doesn't know what to say. Then he offers, "Report cards were mailed. I promise that when you get out, I'll tutor you in trig, and next semester you'll ace the class."

"Thanks," I say. If only Henry knew that trig is the least of my worries. Life is so strange. It once was my biggest worry—that and insomnia and my mom. And now it's *way* far down on my list. Survival has moved to the top.

"Henry and I need to go. Aphrodite says you have to rest. Doctor's orders. She promised to call me if there is any change. My parents will probably come during visiting hours tomorrow. My mom and dad are worried *sick* about you. They said if you need anything . . ."

"Thanks," I whisper. I've lost about twenty-four hours. I think of my mother and Grandpa and Sebastian. What have those twenty-four hours been like for them?

Henry and Annie leave the room. I look around. I'm in a private room with a rose-covered border print about halfway up the drab cream-colored walls. Next to my bed is a faux-leather sleeper chair, with a blanket and a pillow on it. I guess my father and Aphrodite took turns keeping watch. There are flowers in vases—hyacinth and lilies of the valley and orchids, nothing ordinary. And snow globes are lined up on the windowsill. Clearly, Aphrodite has taken control of decorating.

My eyelids flutter. I fight it. But the medication is powerful. I feel as if I'm underwater. A numbness settles over me, a warm wash of well-being, but I know that's the medication. My mind is screaming, *Get up.* But I cannot stay awake. I shut my eyes, then force them open again. If I go to the Underworld now, I will have even less control and power.

I will not fall asleep, I say. I mutter it to myself, but then I realize I just think I'm saying the words. I'm actually just moving my lips with no sound coming out.

I can't focus my pupils. And slowly, my world goes black.

I am in the hallway of many doors. The sconces are no longer here. It's darker than it's ever been.

I squint to try to orient myself. I feel as if my legs are made of spaghetti. I stumble along, searching for something, as if I have misplaced . . . my keys!

I look down, and they are in my hand. I feel feverish. My cheeks are burning. The doors swim before my eyes, as if the entire hall is a mirage in a sandy desert, the dance of heat delusions, the shimmer of a false oasis.

I try to walk, but I stumble. Finally, I sit down on the floor. . . . I lean my head back against the cool rock. I press my cheek to it, grateful for its chilly surface.

I just need to rest. Just for a minute. Just for a minute . . .

And then I hear it.

Muffled. Far-off.

My mother's voice, calling for me.

I try to stand, but my knees are too wobbly. I first clamber onto all fours, then, slowly and agonizingly, I pull myself up, inch by inch, hanging on to a doorknob and clawing my way upright.

I'm coming, I mouth. Why can't I speak? Mommy, I'm coming.

But I realize I am not actually talking.

I lean against the wall for support and move in shuffling steps down the hall. I lean my face against each door, listening, resting, trying to remain upright.

Finally, I arrive at the door I think my mother is behind. It is completely nondescript. A door like any door.

"Mommy?" I breathe. "Are you okay?"

The voice comes through the door. "Iris? Yes, Grandpa and I are fine."

"Thank God."

"Can you open the door? Get us out of here."

My head swims. I realize I can no longer move my hands. Nothing works. My fingers won't cooperate.

I'm so sorry, Mommy.

I think the words, but I don't say them.

I feel as if someone is drawing thick velvet curtains in front of my eyes.

And then the hallway of many doors goes completely black.

17

*We always know when we are awake that
we cannot be dreaming even though when
actually dreaming we feel all this may be real.*

RUTH RENDELL

ris?" Morpheus is sitting in the chair beside my bed.
"Iris? Wake up."

I feel his strong hand on my shoulder. I open my
eyes.

"You were tossing and turning. And moaning in
your sleep, my sweet girl. Do you need your nurse?"

I groan. "I need to go *back*."

"You went to the Underworld?"

I nod. "Mom is there. In the hallway of many
doors."

He swallows. He leans his head closer to me,
pressing his forehead almost to mine. "Is she . . . ?"

He exhales to gather himself and chokes on the next word. "Okay?"

I am struck that he is a god, but he is also so . . . human in a way.

"She said she was. That she and Grandpa were together. I didn't get to see her. She was behind a door. She asked me to unlock it. I . . . I passed out." My failure weighs on me. "I'm so sorry."

"Do not apologize. Do not. This is not your doing." He exhales again. "The hallway is endless. The dream doors as infinite as the dreamers themselves."

"But you're the god of dreams. Go there and find her. Can't you tell which door?"

"Epiales is playing a game. That door is part of your nightmare realm. It's not *my* door. He's a clever one, my devious brother. He'll hide her in a nightmare. If we could get to that door again, we could get her and your grandfather back. If we can rescue them, Epiales will be furious. He'll come here to the mortal world to try to seize them again. He's more vulnerable here. We can definitely defeat him."

"Get Dr. Koios. Bring him here. I can find her and Grandpa. I can do it." My eyes sting. I wonder about Sebastian, too.

His face grows stern. "No. I have every member of my influence searching for them—and Sebastian.

He's headstrong. My guess is he's trying to cross the River of Sorrows to reach you, Iris. I have as many men as I can spare combing the banks of the river. They'll enter the Underworld's city gates and appeal to Hades on his throne. Now that I at least know your mother is unharmed, she will be found. I will go there myself. Epiales must be stopped. He's gone too far this time."

My gut throbs like I have a heartbeat there, then a shooting, stabbing pain attacks my upper-left abdomen—where my spleen is located. I know I need more pain medication soon.

"I found her because I'm your daughter."

"I know—"

"No." I try to raise myself up. It hurts too much. I press the Call button for my nurse. But I have to help him understand.

"Listen to me . . ." I swallow. "Dad."

His eyes well at the word.

"I found her because I am *your* daughter, and I go to the Underworld, the netherworld, that dreamworld, when I dream. But I also found her because I am *her* daughter. I am bonded to her. All my life, she and Grandpa . . . and later Annie . . . they were all I had. I understand how this is so complicated. I don't blame you. But the fact is, Mom, Grandpa, and I are closer than most. I found her because of who I am. Part of *both* of you." When I say it, I feel as if I finally understand who I am. I am no longer the daughter of some anonymous donor. I have *two* parents.

My nurse, Gladys, comes in with my pain shot. She smiles at my father and puts the shot into my IV line.

"Do you need anything else? Some ice chips?"

I shake my head.

My nurse checks all my IVs, presses a button on one machine, and leaves, turning off the overhead light on the way out. Morpheus leans back in the chair. I see the storms flashing in his eyes in the dimness of the room.

The medication fog settles over me, taking the edge off my pain.

"Please," I say to him, before I return to my drug-induced sleep. "Let me go back. Bring Dr. Koios. I'll find them."

He takes one of my hands and strokes the back of it with his fingers. He turns it over and kisses my palm. Then he squeezes it and simply holds it in his. I marvel that he is here. And for the first time in my entire life, I fall asleep holding my dad's hand.

∞

When I wake up again, Aphrodite is in my room,

along with Dr. Koios and my father. I have lost all track of time, but outside the window it is pitch-black, a sprinkling of stars in the sky.

"She's awake." Aphrodite sighs. She sits down on my bed and puts a hand to my forehead. "Her fever is down."

She immediately pulls a hairbrush out and starts gently working through my curls. Then she gets a washcloth and a basin of warm water. She washes my face and my neck. I decide that she and Nico should have a baby. She is definitely mom material.

I wonder what the nurses think of Aunt Aphrodite. She's wearing the proverbial "little black cocktail dress," with black seamed stockings and a pair of Louboutins. I can see the red on the sole when she crosses her legs. A single strand of pearls encircles her neck. I guess this is her attempt to tone it down, though I can't help but notice she has on a massive diamond and sapphire ring—bigger than Princess Diana's famous one, and three blingy bracelets on her wrist. I guess she can't help herself.

But at least she's left the tiara at home.

I look up at Morpheus. "Are you going to let me go back?"

He nods reluctantly. "With me."

"And me," says Aphrodite.

"And me," says Dr. Koios.

"How is that possible?"

"I am Morpheus." My father smiles, as if that is the simplest explanation in the world, and no more is necessary. "You aren't going back alone. I cannot allow it. But I recognize your wisdom. You have the connection to them. You will be able to discern where they are faster than even I. The land of dreams is vast—almost infinite. The land of nightmares equally so. And Epiales is hiding them in your nightmares." For the first time, I see the weight of his universe on his face, the vast responsibility of controlling the kingdom of dreams. Of warring with the prince of nightmares.

"Okay," I breathe.

"How is your pain?" Aunt Aphrodite asks me.

"Hurts." But if I'm going to go there and not collapse in the hallway, I need to put off my pain medication. So I manage a smile. "But not as bad."

"Your white counts are still sky-high. Your spleen is still swollen. You will be very careful," Dr. Koios says.

Morpheus nods. "If Koios says it is time for us to leave, then it is time for us to leave. I won't lose . . ." He looks away and can't finish the sentence.

"Okay." But deep down, I know I'm not leaving without my mother and Grandpa.

Aphrodite goes to the door of my hospital room. They have chosen a time between rounds when the patients are supposed to be asleep. She shuts my door.

The three of them stand around my bed. We all hold hands and form a circle of sorts. Dr. Koios tells me, "Pain can take you out of deep relaxation. Just concentrate on my voice."

"See you on the other side." Morpheus grins at me. I think it is the first time I have seen his smile. His eyes flash in a different way.

As usual, Dr. Koios urges me into deeper relaxation. I find the beeping of my IVs distracting, and my skin crawls, like thousands of little bugs are skittering up my arms, thanks to my medication, so I have to concentrate harder than usual.

I am in the hallway of many doors. The sconces are there. I smile. Next to me are Dr. Koios, Morpheus, and Aphrodite.

"We'll follow your lead," Dr. Koios says.

We walk down the hallway, and I pause. I press my hands on different doors. Sometimes it is easy to decide, because I have Morpheus with me.

"Not that one," he says, shaking his head when I touch a door that is the precise shade of a brilliant cardinal.

"Why not?"

"That's a recurring dream. Flying."

We get a little farther, and he points out other doors we can skip. Teeth falling out. Being naked in front of a roomful of people. Being in trig class and being unprepared for a test. I have that one a lot. Missing a plane.

We walk past the recurring dreams. Then he shows me some of my old dream doors.

"This one was the time you dreamed that you were a mermaid and could swim underwater."

I smile at the memory. I always liked that one.

Aphrodite has her hand at the small of my spine, and she keeps patting me reassuringly. I feel so much more secure with them here.

We keep walking until I feel a pain in my side.

"Can we rest a moment?"

The four of us stop. From far down the tunnel, I hear growls. I look up at Morpheus.

He shakes his head. "They wouldn't dare. Not with me here."

I feel another stabbing pain. "Dr. Koios . . ." My breath is knocked out of me. The hallway looks hazy, and I am afraid I'm losing consciousness.

He feels my head. "I think she's spiking a fever again. We should—"

"No, I won't leave—we're too close."

I turn my head to look back where we came, and I let out a little scream. Thousands of cockroaches are crawling on the walls, a horrifying wave of bugs, like living wallpaper. I feel them on my skin, but when I look down at my arms, nothing is there. I'm losing my mind.

Aphrodite shrieks and starts hopping from foot to foot on her stilettos. "I hate bugs," she says. "Morpheus . . . please . . ." She hides behind him, standing on tiptoe and peeking over his shoulder before burying her face against his back.

But Morpheus steps toward the bugs. He stares down the hallway and his eyes flash lightning inside them. The flames from the sconces grow larger. The flames flicker and dance, then lick the walls. Fire escapes the sconces and continues sliding down the walls, incinerating the bugs. The hallway smells singed. Black, acrid smoke lingers. I cough.

Speak to me, Mom. I want to get out of here.

Then I have another thought. Maybe I am going at this the wrong way. If I were Epiales, where would I hide them?

"Of course," I breathe. I try to walk, but the pain is too intense. "I know where they are." My knees buckle, and Morpheus and Dr. Koios support me on each side. I still can't walk on.

"Carry me," I say to Morpheus.

He scoops me into his arms as if I were light as a rag doll.

"Take me to the airport."

"The what?"

"The recurring dream—the one where you miss your plane."

We go back the way we came, and I feel as if my world is turning black. "Faster!" I urge. "We don't have a lot of time."

The keys are in my hand. I pass the ring to Aphrodite. "The one that's hot will open it."

She touches them, running her fingers over them. She shakes her head. "You have to, Iris. They're your keys."

I struggle, hands shaking. I find a key with a sleek line to it. I hand it to Dr. Koios. "Open the door."

He does, and when we step through, we are in a crowded airport. But all the announcements say "Final boarding," and all the electronic boards read DEPARTED. Every plane is a missed connection.

And there, sitting at Gate 112B, suitcases around them, are my mother and Grandpa.

"How did you know?" Aphrodite asks, baffled.

"Easy," I say. "I've never had this dream. It would be the last place I'd look."

My mother and grandfather see us in the throngs of travelers. Tears streaming down her face, Mom *leaps from her seat and runs to me, Grandpa right behind her.*

They both try to hug me in Morpheus's arms.

"Why are you carrying her?" she asks my father.

She presses her hand to my forehead. "Oh my God, Iris. Dad, she's sick."

"Grandpa . . . Mommy . . ." The words flutter on my lips, and then I scream in pain, just before falling unconscious.

*People who are most afraid of their dreams
convince themselves they don't dream at all.*

JOHN STEINBECK

I lose two days of my life.

I remember waking and then falling into unconsciousness. Waking and falling, falling and waking. I remember spinning, the room whirling around me as if I was in the eye of a tornado.

I remember faces.

Aphrodite and Nico, Dr. Koios, Annie, Henry Wu, Annie's mom and dad, Grandpa, and Mom. And my father. Their faces came to me in hazy images, like looking through eighteenth-century glass. I remember the doctor asking me to do things, like lift my index finger or blink my eyes.

But I couldn't even open my eyes. I would tell myself to open my eyes, but my body betrayed me.

My eyes wouldn't listen. My index finger wouldn't lift. I sank deeper and deeper into illness.

Mostly, I remember voices.

My mother and father and Grandpa pleading with me to get well.

Aphrodite crying. I remember her tears splashing onto my own cheeks as she leaned over to kiss me.

And Annie. I remember her crying. And Henry Wu standing next to her, promising her that somehow, someway, I would survive. And that he would be here for her, no matter what. Forever.

But all the voices of the people I love weren't enough. The medication wasn't enough. I wanted to fight, but my fight was exhausted.

I knew my father was searching everywhere for Sebastian, was searching the River of Sorrows, casting nets, dragging the river for his body, sending out spies against his brother. As I would sink into the darkness, I kept waiting for my angel's voice to call to me, to tell me to fight. I kept waiting to see him in this strange netherworld where I lingered, in the netherworld where I dreamed, but his voice never came.

And then suddenly, here, now, on the third day, I bolt upright in my hospital bed and look out the window into the parking lot. I feel healed, like stones have lifted from my chest. Fine, actually, as if I had never been sick. In the time I have been unconscious, winter has arrived for sure, frost creating a pattern on my hospital window. I think back to the last days I can remember. How much time has passed? I wonder how soon it will be until Christmas.

I take a deep breath. I do not feel any pain. I touch my own forehead. It is cool. I feel along my belly, even pressing in near my spleen. Nothing hurts.

"It's gone!"

My father, who is dozing softly in a chair next to my mother, their hands entwined, her head on his shoulder, opens his eyes. He leans over to kiss her on the top of her head. "Sofia, she's awake."

My mother's eyes spring open, and then just as instantly, they are full of tears. At the sight of me sitting up, her tears rapidly turn to loud, messy sobbing.

"I'm okay, Mom. I'm okay. I promise."

She waves her hands at the air. "I know. It's relief. Relief."

My father presses his fingertips to my forehead. "She's completely cool."

"And your stomach?" Mom asks through sniffles.

"Nothing. No pain."

"Thank God," Mom says. Then she looks at my father. "Thank the gods."

My father presses the Call button for my nurse. She races in. I tell her I feel totally well.

She shakes her head in amazement. "We almost lost you last night. Your fever was teetering to one oh six. Your counts were worse. . . . Let me call the doctor."

She walks over and quickly checks all my IVs. As she turns to leave, she smiles. "Sometimes miracles happen. Best part of my job."

My mother says, "I'll call Aphrodite and Koi and Grandpa."

"Hand me my phone, Mom," I say. "I want to call Annie myself."

As soon as she hears my voice, clear and steady, Annie says she'll be right over. "I just have to find someone to watch the Tiny Terrors. My mom is Christmas shopping."

"Don't worry. Come later. I'm okay. I swear. Pinkie promise. Cross my heart and hope to . . . Nah, forget that. Just promise. I really and truly am all better."

All afternoon and into early evening, a parade of doctors and specialists poke and prod me. They murmur and furrow their brows, looking very serious, wondering how I could have made such a startling recovery. Vials of blood are taken. Aphrodite and Nico come to visit. Grandpa does, too, and after a hug so big I think my ribs are bruised, he becomes so choked up he has to leave the room.

Dr. Bingham says there's no explanation. Not a logical one, at least. Every level in my blood is normal. My spleen is back to the size it should be. But she won't release me until I eat food and don't relapse. Twenty-four hours more, at least. I am aching to leave. And as relieved as I am to be well, and for my mom and grandfather to be okay, my mind turns to Sebastian.

My mother looks exhausted. I send her and my father down to the cafeteria to get coffee. He's tireless. A god. But she is mortal, and the stress is showing. But at least she's awake.

I am sitting cross-legged in my bed, clicking through the TV channels, when Annie and Henry arrive. She throws herself on me in the bed. We hug for a long time. Then she kisses me on the top of my head and climbs off and stands next to Henry.

"Please tell me this is all over." She waves her hands around wildly.

I don't know whether she means Epiales or my illness or what. But Henry is here, so I can't go into detail. Love agrees with him. His hair is combed in a cool new style—I think he's even got a little gel in it. He looks different somehow.

More confident. Not the boy who looked as if he was going to hurl his lunch because Annie talked to him. With him here, though, I can't ask Annie exactly what she means.

"I told Henry," Annie says. "Everything."

"What do you mean, everything. Ev-er-y-thing?" I ask, thinking Annie is being Annie and maybe she's a tiny bit confused.

"No. Everything. You know. My best friend is a goddess. Half goddess. Demi-goddess. Whatever."

My eyes widen.

"And he *believed* you?" My eyebrows shoot up. This is Henry. Smartest guy in our school. That he hasn't run off thinking we're both insane *must* mean he is a soul-mate match.

"Well"—Henry grins—"I have to admit, when she was first talking about stigmata on your ankles, I was confused."

"But then I told him about Aphrodite."

"And then we had our first kiss."

"And definitely top-twenty material," Annie blurts out.

Henry blushes.

"So spill, is it over?" she asks.

"Epiales won't give up. I guess that Morpheus, my

dad, thinks now that Mom and Grandpa are rescued, Epiales will come back to this realm again. Whatever his plan was, whatever was meant about my being a 'pawn,' Epiales won't give up. He'll be back. But at least here, in the mortal world, he's weaker. Better to face him here than in the Underworld." I don't add that I'm terrified of what that'll mean for us in this world.

And then the door to my room opens.

And Sebastian walks in.

And despite being well, I almost faint.

He looks battered and bruised. His face is pale, and he has the shadow of stubble across his cheeks and chin, which looks hot.

I can't even speak, I am so shocked. I want to pinch myself, to make sure that this isn't some sick dream, that this is reality. Before I can he races to my bed and kneels next to it, wrapping his arms around me. I *feel* his arms around me. In this world. In *my* world. He is flesh and blood.

My heartbeat increases, and he raises himself up and sits on my bed and kisses me. I touch my fingers to his lips, trembling. This is real. And I know what Aphrodite says, but if our kiss isn't number one, it is in the top ten.

He pulls away. Annie and Henry stare at him.

"Is this . . . ?" she asks.

I nod.

"I so totally get why you would go to the Underworld for him."

Sebastian smiles and kisses my hand. "Annie?" he asks, cocking his head toward her.

She nods.

"We've met in her dreams. Not that you'd remember, since it was in Iris's head."

Henry sticks out his hand. "I'm Henry."

My father and mother walk in, followed by Aphrodite. The three of them stare at Sebastian. He immediately stands and bows to my father. "Prince Morpheus . . ."

My father shakes his head, as if to say the formality isn't necessary. "You crossed. That's why she's well. You managed to cross the river."

Sebastian nods.

In his beautiful voice, the voice of my dreams, he tells us the story. "I was determined to be with Iris here. To protect her from Epiales. To never leave her side. But to become mortal, I had to cross the River of Sorrows. And the Ferryman said only by surviving your worst nightmare do you manage to cross the river and not end up in Tartarus."

"What's that?" Henry asks.

"A dungeon below even the Underworld, where you suffer for all eternity."

I look at my father. The gods *certainly* like dramatics.

"When did you enter the river?" Morpheus questions.

"Four days ago. Under cover of night, I waded in. As soon as my body entered the water, I had flashes of Iris in pain. The images tormented me. I didn't think she was going to survive, and I blamed myself. I thought my worst nightmare would be *my* torture. But I'd already suffered that. And I should have known. Should have anticipated Epiales's brutality."

Sebastian grows quiet for a moment. Then he whispers, "At night I would hear Epiales's voice. He would tell me everything he was going to do to you, Iris, how you would suffer. He offered me a bargain. If I went to Tartarus forever, he would release you from your pain. I was drowning, literally, in the River of Sorrows, sucking in black water. I looked up at the black sky and saw you, in this hospital bed, dying."

"But you're here," Aphrodite murmurs. "How . . . ?"

"I was ready to accept the deal. I didn't know if he would keep his promise, but . . . I couldn't imagine a worse torture than watching Iris die. I was willing to take the risk. And no sooner had I opened my mouth, ready to accept, that I felt a rock beneath my foot. I had somehow made it to the other side. I fought to get to the shore, the last yards just crawling against the tide, but eventually, I threw myself on the bank. And I passed out."

"And my illness lifted."

He nods.

Everyone visits for a while. Then the nurse says visiting hours are over. She steps out of the room so we all can say our good-byes.

My father's forehead furrows. "I don't know where to be tonight. With your mother . . . or here. I'll feel better when you're all in one house again."

"I'll stay," Sebastian offers. Inside I am elated.

My parents nod. It's weird to see them as a couple. It's weird to see my mother awake.

One by one, they each lean down for a kiss. Aphrodite hugs me to her breast. "There's baklava with your name on it when you get home."

Then it's just Sebastian and me.

I still can't believe he's here.

My nurse pokes her head in and sees him in the chair next to the bed. It's past visiting hours. I think she's going to tell him to leave, since he's not my mom or my dad. Instead, she whispers, "After all you've been through, I'll look the other way tonight." She winks and then says to Sebastian, "Just make sure she gets her rest or she won't be released tomorrow."

The hospital floor grows quiet. I click off the TV, which has been on in the background all this time. By the rail of my bed, I press on the Light button until my room is almost dark, just a soft night-light on.

Sebastian moves from the chair to the edge of my bed. "I can't believe I'm here." He puts his hands to either side of my face. "I don't know what I would have done if . . ." Rather than finish the sentence, he kisses me.

He slides down until he is lying next to me. I shift in the bed to make room. He kisses my neck. Then he lies on his back. I roll on my side and settle into the crook of his arm. I touch his skin, the stubble on his chin. I wrap my fingers in his curls, still not believing he is here. I touch his bruises. "Sebastian . . ."

"Worth every sacrifice."

I nestle in. I love the *feel* of him in real life. I inhale. He still smells like the sea, the way I remember it from my dreams.

His breathing grows steady. I look at him, and he is

sound asleep, his long lashes like feathers, his profile strong.

And for the first time, for as long as I can remember, I fall asleep peacefully.

I am so relieved to be home. The first thing I do is take a long, hot shower. I am shocked when I look in the mirror. My face is thin, and deep circles rest in the hollows beneath my eyes—worse than usual. I dress in yoga pants and a sweatshirt, shaking a little. I still can't believe Sebastian is mortal, and that he is *here* in my house. This feels like a dream, but it's real. Usually my dreams feel real, but they are mirages that slip through my fingers.

When I go out to the living room, everyone is there, and they cheer when they see me. Grandpa has ordered takeout from no fewer than three restaurants—including a new Greek place we're trying—and has set the dining room table up like a buffet—with our good china and silver. Aphrodite has apparently had Nico bring candelabras from her house. Ornate baroque angels hold up tapered candles. Aphrodite pours wine for her, Grandpa, Dr. Koios, Nico, and my parents; Henry, Sebastian, Annie, and I settle on the carpet around the coffee table to eat our food and drink our sodas.

Sebastian lifts an eyebrow at the snow globes.

I look around. Aphrodite is in the kitchen—I can hear her flirting with Nico. Since she's out of earshot, I whisper, "These aren't usually here. Grandpa hates clutter. They're Aphrodite's."

"What are they?"

Henry, Annie, and I stare at him. Annie freezes, a piece of pizza halfway to her mouth.

"Snow globes," Henry says.

"You know, sno-o-o-o-w gl-o-o-o-bes," Annie repeats slowly, stretching both words out, and putting the slice of pizza down on her plate.

"You said that." He laughs softly.

"I thought just in case you mostly speak ancient Greek or something."

"Annie"—I sigh—"you've talked to him before. You know he speaks English."

"An Annie-ism." Henry smiles and looks at her adoringly.

I look at the snow globe and then stare at Sebastian strangely. I realize he has lived in my dreams. He has never been to school. Or eaten pizza. Or experienced Red Bull. Or, like Aphrodite, had a sleepover and watched movies all night. Or done any of the things that Henry, Annie, and I have.

Henry gives Annie a little elbow. I think he's realized it, too. And then Annie's eyes get that I-get-it look.

I lift a snow globe—one of Aphrodite's prettiest ones. Inside are two traditional Greek dancers, a boy and a girl. On the bottom is a winding mechanism. I wind it, and tinny Greek music plays. I shake up the snow globe really hard with two hands and set it down directly in front of Sebastian. Inside the two little figures twirl in a circle, and the music plays while snow rains down on them.

His face is transformed. He's so sexy and masculine, but for the moment, he looks like an innocent boy, like the boy in the tree house who wanted to play pirates. When the snow globe stops, he grins. "Do it again?"

I wind it up, and he is just as captivated. He takes it in his hands and holds it even closer. My heart just melts like a slushie.

Everyone is now in the living room. Aphrodite starts crying over her souvlaki.

"What?" I ask. "Everything is okay now." Well, at least sort of okay.

Nico immediately runs to get her tissues and kneels down and dabs at her face, brushing aside a stray hair and fixing her tiara.

"It's not that"—she sniffles—"I just got used to being here. To being a *thia*—an auntie. And now I have to go home."

"Well, you're *still* my auntie," I say.

"But I'm all the way out in *Queens*." She says Queens like it's three syllables.

"We'll visit on weekends. Family dinners on Sundays," I offer, exchanging a look with Mom and then Grandpa, hoping that's okay.

"Absolutely!" he exclaims.

I exhale, relieved. I didn't know how he felt about gaining a goddess in the family. Particularly one who cluttered up his house beyond recognition.

"We're family," my mother says. She gets up and walks over to Aphrodite and kisses her on the cheek.

We all stay up late. Henry and Annie, Sebastian and I go into my room. We show Sebastian YouTube and give him a crash course in modern teenage life. He loves the Mentos-in-soda trick. And our modern music.

Around eleven thirty, Henry looks at the time on my computer. "I better go. Curfew."

"Drive me home?" Annie asks him. She looks at me. "I'd stay, but my mom needs me to babysit the Tiny Terrors in the morning. She's got to take my dad's mom to my aunt's house upstate. Gram's going to stay with my aunt Jackie for Christmas. We've had her since Thanksgiving. And I have to tell you, Mom loves Gram, but she is so ready to have her kitchen back to herself."

Henry and Annie stand. He looks at me. "I'm really, really glad you're okay, Iris."

"Thanks, Henry."

"Promise you . . . we'll get you an A in trig."

"I'd settle for a B-minus."

"Deal." He looks me in the eyes. His are moist. "You really scared Annie. I'm so glad there's a happy ending."

A happy ending for now. It never is far from my mind that it isn't *over*. That Epiales will not be happy Morpheus outwitted him and we got my mom and Grandpa back again. Epiales will be coming. And though I feel a *lot* better with Morpheus and Aphrodite and Koios—and Sebastian—on my side, I'm not sure a celebration is completely in order. Despite the wonderful night we all enjoyed.

Henry smiles and sticks out his hand. "It's been

great meeting you, Sebastian. I guess we'll be seeing a lot of you."

Sebastian nods and shakes his hand.

It's then that I sort of wonder what, precisely, we *are* going to do with Sebastian. He has no past, no identification, no family. I'm his only tie to this world. Forget trig—he's never even been in a classroom. I decide we'll figure it out later.

Annie hugs me and then Sebastian.

"I'll call you tomorrow," she says. "Maybe we can go to the movies."

As they leave, Mom comes in.

"Aphrodite and Nico have the guest room. Sebastian can bunk in with Grandpa if he wants. Once Aphrodite moves out, he can take her room. Or I'm more than happy to make up the sofa bed in the office on the second floor. You know, maybe that would be better anyway. Sebastian, you'd have more privacy. The mattress is a little lumpy, but it's just for a couple of nights."

"That sounds great."

Mom goes to fix up his room. Sebastian faces me. He reaches out and plays with my hair, wrapping a curl around his index finger. "I can't believe I'm here, touching you."

I realize I can't even articulate how unbelievable this is. All of it. But then, I didn't become mortal.

"Regrets?"

"None."

I touch one of his bruises. "These don't heal so fast here."

"That's okay. I can do this here." And he leans over and kisses me, and I feel my insides melt into a puddle.

I sigh. Life is kind of working out. I'm hopeful with Morpheus around that my mom is over her sleeping illness. I have the man of my dreams. Annie has Henry. Now if only Epiales would stay away.

Mom pokes her head in. "I left a toothbrush and toothpaste on your bed. The bathroom is across the hall."

He stands, kisses the top of my head, and says, softly, "Good night."

I change into my pajamas and then settle into bed. I stare at the ceiling. I realize I will no longer have Sebastian's voice to guide me. My dreams will somehow be lonelier. But now that I know how to lucidly dream, now that I know my own power, now that I have met my father, I think that maybe, at last, I can sleep and dream like a normal person.

But my insomnia remains. I toss and turn. I think about Sebastian. He's right upstairs. I consider sneaking up there. But *he* needs to sleep. He's mortal now, and he needs to heal. Plus, for the first time my *dad* is in my house. I realize I can get in trouble now. Like he might ground me if I get caught. I smile at the idea. Grandpa and Mom have spoiled me my whole life. And I'm basically a good kid—Annie and I have been to parties and stuff, but . . . we've just never been the kind to do things to get ourselves grounded. She's always been focused on getting a soccer scholarship. And I just never had a reason to do anything crazy. But now Annie and I both have boyfriends. I wonder if that's all about to change. Then again, Henry wanted to get home before curfew. So maybe not.

Thinking about the *kind* of trouble I can get in with Sebastian makes me laugh to myself. I take my iPod from my nightstand, pop in the earbuds, and click on my classical music playlist. At the soft music of *Nocturnes*, I finally feel sleepy.

I am in the hallway of many doors. I look down at my hands. I do not have my key ring. I approach the first door I see. But with no key, how can I open the lock?

The door is made of bamboo reeds. I touch the handle. I find that the knob turns. I smile. Own your power, Iris. I can now open the doors without a key. All my dreaming doors are unlocked.

I walk into the dreaming room. It's a beach. Someplace like Fiji. I'm dressed in a bikini. I walk on soft white sand, warm to my feet but not hot, to the water's edge. The water crests and waves crash softly at my feet, ribbons of foam dancing around me. I wade in to my waist, the sun kissing my face. The water is so clear, I can see tropical fish darting and dashing around me. A blue angelfish comes so close, I think it would let me touch it if I dared.

I sink down into the water and start to float. I turn around and see Sebastian on the shore. His voice no longer leads me, but I can still dream about him.

He wades into the water and swims to me. He dives underwater and playfully grabs my legs, surfaces, and says, "I'm a shark."

Standing up, he kisses me. I love the feeling of our wet bodies pressed together.

I look at the horizon. It's nearly sunset, the sun an orange glowing ball, sinking into the sea.

We watch it dip below our line of sight and then we walk out of the water. A blanket is on the beach, and we sit on it, his arm around me. Everything is perfect.

Only suddenly, I can't breathe. I look at Sebastian with terror on my face. I am suffocating. An unseen attacker's hands are around my throat.

I bolt awake. My room is dark, which isn't how I left it. I look over at my computer. The power is off. It's then I realize the house is completely silent. No central heat running in the chilly December night. No sounds. Our power is out.

I put my hands to my neck, trying to reassure myself that I'm okay, trying to steady my breathing. But I have the creeping realization that someone is in my room.

Fighting panic, I scream for my father, but a man's hand slips over my mouth.

"Quiet, Iris, you wouldn't want to wake Daddy now, would you?" In the darkness, I see two eyes, glowing slightly, and they are stormy mirrors. Epiales.

He rips me from my bed, pulling me hard and fast and dragging me along the floor. His arms are so powerful that my feet are two inches off the floor, my toes barely scraping the carpet. He opens my bedroom door, hauls me down the hallway, and tosses me into the living room. In the living room, by the faint light from the window, I see another figure dressed in black. He has my aunt tied to a chair. Nico is lying unconscious—or dead—on the floor. I would expect Aunt Aphrodite to be crying, but instead, it's like watching fireworks on the Fourth of July. Her eyes are sparking continuously with her fury.

Epiales sneers. "Always such a hothead, Aphrodite, dear. You should learn to control that temper of yours."

"You wait. You'll wish for death, you bastard. You'll wish you were mortal so your pain can end."

In another minute, Grandpa is there, roused from sleep, white hair a fright—he needs a haircut—Yankees shirt and boxers on. I am so thankful Annie didn't sleep over, and that Dr. Koios—though I've taken to calling him Uncle Koi now—drove home to Jersey.

That leaves just my mother and father and Sebastian to be dragged into this nightmare—only it's not a nightmare. I just wish that it was.

But an unfamiliar male voice shouts from back near my mother's bedroom, "Morpheus and his woman are not in the bed!"

"Impossible!" Epiales shouts back. He pulls a black gun from his waistband and hands it to his henchman. "If any of them move, use it." Then he runs toward my mom's bedroom.

When he comes back, the rage is evident. His mirrorlike eyes are glowing and flashing. I can sense the hatred and tension mounting. The air is so electric between the immortals that I'm sure if a match was lit, the room would erupt into flames.

Epiales runs to Aphrodite. He grabs her face. "Tell me where they are."

She spits in his face.

He slaps her.

"Tell me or the next bit of pain I deliver will be to your precious niece."

Her eyes glow in the dimness. "I have no idea. And Hades may protect you now, but when Zeus finds out that you have dared to lay a hand on me, you will wish yourself in Tartarus. You will *beg* to be there to end your suffering. You will wish to drown in the River Styx."

Suddenly, in through the front door bursts my father, four soldiers I have never seen before, and Sebastian. They are dressed in black sweaters and black pants, black fisherman caps on their heads.

A gun goes off, and I scream and crouch down behind a chair. I hear crashing and punches being thrown and landing. Sebastian throws one of Epiales's soldiers against the bookcase, and the entire thing falls on top of them, books flying and Aphrodite's knickknacks breaking. She's going to be even more angry. It's a wonder anything in my living room has survived these last weeks.

Then Epiales grabs me, pulls me to my feet, and holds a knife to my throat. I feel the blade slice my skin slightly, feel the warmth of my own blood in the faintest of trickles.

"Stop!" My father orders his men to hold back. His eyes flash, and I feel heat emanating from him, warming the chilly room.

"That's more like it," Epiales says.

I can see Sebastian's face—he's seething.

"Release her. Or there will be war, Epiales. Hades and Zeus will not approve," Morpheus commands.

"There won't be a war. This ends here. Relinquish your realm to me."

I swallow. That's what they meant about my being a pawn. I knew it was more than my humanity he hated. He wanted something. My father's world. This has all been about the power.

"Never, brother."

"Oh, you *will* hand me the keys to your realm. You're so foolish, Morpheus. The first time I saw her in the Underworld, when I realized who she was, I celebrated. You, the mighty Morpheus, have a weakness. And not just any weakness. A *woman* first, and then lo and behold, a daughter."

Epiales laughs like a madman. "What a fool you are. A balance of power between dreams and nightmares has existed since the dawn of time, and there was not a crack to be had, nothing for me to use to change that. And then you, Morpheus, you showed your Achilles' heel."

I realize Epiales and Morpheus know the *real* Achilles.

"There is a reason we don't associate with mortals anymore, Morpheus. That's so we don't *long* for their lives. That we don't find ourselves torn by the decisions we must make—torn by *sentiment*." He spits the word. "Sentiment. You disgust me. Here you are, you a *god*, heartbroken over a woman. Do you know how pathetic that is? We are *gods. Gods!* And nothing should be more important to us than ruling. Than power. Than our realms. Not a woman, and *most* especially, not your daughter—who shouldn't even exist!"

"Release her." My father's voice is steady.

"You know, I could have killed her before. It wouldn't have been hard at all—these mortals die so easily. But it is *so* much better this way. This has been absolutely simple. And fun. Truly fun."

"Epiales, I'm warning you." Morpheus's eyes are flashing, lighting the room.

"Yes, well, to just kill her and take your realm would incite war. Hades and Zeus would not approve. But if you *gave* me your realm, gave it to me of your own free will . . . now, who can argue with that? So it was better to lure you to your poor defenseless child who was in danger. A child who didn't even know who her daddy was. A child in turmoil and confusion. After all these centuries, I know you so well, brother."

I hate hearing him tormenting my father like this.

"I watched you these years. The time has flown by like *minutes* in terms of an immortal. I stood by patiently and watched as you protected her, kept vigil over her. Your judgment was impaired. You started to believe you could have both a mortal family *and* a realm in the netherworld. You *cannot* have both! I will make the choice simple for you: give me your realm. And you can have your family. Alive."

"Don't, Morpheus." I find my voice. He can't. He can't let Epiales rule the mortal world's subconscious and turn every night, every dream, into a nightmare.

"You can't be a part of my life, Morpheus. I don't want you here, I don't want you as a father." I know how much my father has given up for me, how devoted he is to me. So my only choice is to lie. To lie and hope he believes me.

"Shut up!" Epiales presses the knife to my throat. But I know he won't kill me—he can't. If he does, he'll have nothing to bargain with.

"No, Morpheus," I say, "you can't come into my life after almost seventeen years and just pretend, like, now we're a family. What? After this it will go back to the way it was before? You occasionally taking the form of a Santa or a janitor? It wasn't good enough then, and it's not good enough now. Go back to the Underworld where you belong." I practically choke on the words.

"You don't mean that," Aunt Aphrodite says, sniffling from her chair.

"I do." I look directly at Morpheus. "I don't want you—you're no father to me."

My father's face pales, and he clenches his jaw. "Iris . . . you're my *child*."

The pain in his voice rips at me, but I shake my head. "Go back to where you belong. Let me be an ordinary girl. An ordinary fatherless girl. Like I always was."

"Bitch!" Epiales says. He hasn't expected this hand. I smile. He shoves me to the floor and kicks me as hard as he can.

From behind him, my mother—who has come out of nowhere—swings a ceramic lamp down on his head. He barely flinches, but he's distracted long enough for my father to tackle him. They slam into the living room wall, cracking the plaster.

Sebastian says to Epiales's men, and to my father's, "Leave them. This has always been between the brothers. They need to settle it."

One of Epiales's men tries to move, and Sebastian punches him in the jaw. "Leave them," he shouts, "or you will answer to Hades and Zeus."

The soldiers back off. Everyone now watches the fight between the two brothers.

Morpheus and Epiales trade brutal blows. They fall on the coffee table and shatter it—along with some of Aphrodite's beloved snow globes. She shrieks.

Grandpa moves to the front door and opens it. After wrestling and punching each other, Morpheus and Epiales crash through the doorway. They somersault down the stone front steps and land on the lawn. Sebastian, the respective soldiers of dreams and nightmares, and Grandpa and Mom run out. I dash to the kitchen, get a knife, and cut Aphrodite free.

She kneels at Nico's side. He has a massive goose egg on the side of his head, but he's breathing.

"He tried to defend me. God, when he comes to, I'm going to have so much explaining to do."

"He had no idea you were *the* Aphrodite?"

"There never seemed to be a good time to tell him."

"You take care of him." I leave Aphrodite and Nico, and run out of the house.

Morpheus and Epiales are still fighting fiercely. A layer of icy fog surrounds our lawn, shielding the fight from the neighbors in a mist, thank goodness. But I stare up at the sky. Thunder rumbles, and strange flashes cross the blackness. I see a star shoot in an arc across the sky—which should be impossible because we're so close to Manhattan's lights.

I hold my breath, shivering in the December air. Epiales rushes headlong into my father's chest.

I feel helpless. I am also terrified that something will happen to Morpheus before I can tell him I didn't mean what I said. I hope that he knows, that he figured out what I was doing. Grandpa comes and puts his arm around me.

"Your father isn't stupid, Iris. He's an immortal god who has seen everything. He knows."

I lean my head against his shoulder. Grandpa always knows what I'm thinking. Sebastian looks at me from across the way. His eyes say the same thing as Grandpa's.

The battle between the two gods rages, and I start wondering what anyone looking at the night sky will think. Inwardly groaning, I know this is going to make the news. The clouds flash the way my father's eyes do. The way Aphrodite's do. People will think the end of the world is coming. If they only knew the strange truth—that it's the gods.

My father and Epiales are both battered and bloody. Aphrodite and a wobbly Nico come out the front door.

I look up at the strange sky again.

I blink.

There, in among the lightning, is a woman hiding behind a cloud.

20

All men whilst they are awake are in one common
world; but each of them, when he is asleep,
is in a world of his own.

PLUTARCH

Distracted for a moment by the woman in the sky,
I look back at my father and uncle. Morpheus
has Epiales by the throat. And then, in Epiales's hand,
I see a blade.

"Dad, watch! He has a knife!" The blade's brilliant
silver arcs through the air. My father raises his arm—
and I hear his scream as the blade rips into his flesh.
My father staggers backward, stumbles, and falls to
the ground.

I run toward them, as Epiales lifts his knife high,
ready to stab my father in the chest. I know my
father is a god, but he has already told me that his
and Epiales's powers are weaker here.

I fling myself at Epiales. He's done everything he can to destroy me, my father, Sebastian, my life here. I catch him off guard, and he whirls around, the knife dropping from his hand. He takes a swing at me, but I duck and throw myself to the ground, as if I'm sliding into base, and scramble for the knife.

Epiales kicks my arm, and I roll over, pain shooting up toward my shoulder. He grabs the knife, even as I see my father is back on his feet. But Epiales raises the blade again. "It would have been so much simpler if my brother had just given up his kingdom."

I stare up at my uncle, seeing the hatred he has for me in his eyes, the blade's sharp edge, Epiales's mouth twisted into one of his grins. I saved my father. Now he has to know I do love him. But is this really how my life is going to end?

But in a flash, Sebastian comes between Epiales and me.

"No, Iris!"

Sebastian rushes headlong at Epiales. In the same moment, I see the blade aimed straight for Sebastian's chest. And from the sky, a jagged bolt of lightning strikes the earth with a deafening boom right next to me, throwing everyone to the cold ground. I feel the frozen leaves beneath me. The night is bitter and icy. But I cannot see a thing. I cannot hear any sounds. It's as if the world has gone silent and turned to a dark primordial fog.

I smell burned grass and leaves pressed to my face, and when the smoke clears, the woman from the cloud stands in our midst. I turn my head. My father is climbing to his feet. Epiales is, too.

I lift my head, a throbbing pain in my temples. And then I see him. Sebastian is lying . . . dead. The knife in his chest.

"No!" I scream. I clamber up, clawing in his direction. I fling myself down on his body and lay my head on his stomach, which is eerily still. "No! No! No!" I scream until I am hoarse. I feel Aphrodite's hands on my shoulder, trying to pull me away.

"No!" I sob, looking up at her. "No!"

Then I whisper a silent prayer over and over.

Let this be a dream. Let this be a dream. Please, please, let this be a dream.

Everyone is silent around me. Aphrodite waits, but after several moments, she pulls me from his body. "Come here, Iris. Come here."

I stand, my legs wobbly, and bury my head against her shoulder. She whispers, "Maybe all hope is not lost. It's Nyx, your grandmother. Perhaps the most powerful woman in the Underworld." She positions me so I can see my grandmother. My father and Epiales are kneeling before her.

I still can't take it all in. My father rises, clutching his bleeding arm. Epiales is silent.

Nyx is beautiful. Her hair is long and gleaming black, and her gown is night itself, a cloak of stars and midnight that seems to have a life of its own.

Nyx glares at Epiales. She waves her hand as if dismissing him, as she floats toward me, in a walking motion, though I can see her feet do not touch the ground.

"You are Iris," she says, her voice as lyrical as the wind. She touches my cheek, and where her fingertips caress my skin, I feel almost a tingling. Then she puts her fingers beneath my chin, tilts my face upward until I am looking her in the eyes, though tears are still flowing and I am certain I look like a sloppy mess.

"You have my cheekbones." She smiles at me and wipes at my tears. Her touch is electric.

Sweeping away from me, she approaches her two sons.

"Hades is most displeased. Zeus is furious."

Epiales snarls, "Iris should not exist. That has been our agreement for centuries. Morpheus is the one who broke the covenant."

Nyx appears to ponder this.

Above us the sky still rumbles. Clouds roll. Stars shoot.

"But Iris does exist," she says calmly. "What is done, Epiales, is done."

"He should give up his realm. He should give up his realm because he has betrayed his claim to it. His throne should be mine."

"Epiales, you have your realm." The sky grows even more fierce, as if night itself is in turmoil. "This power play is forbidden! *Both of you* will call off your armies. Call off this war between brothers. Immediately."

Epiales's eyes flash.

"You will appear before Hades to answer for this. Both of you. But Epiales, the fault lies at your feet. Any punishment is yours alone to bear."

Morpheus glares at his brother.

He looks back at me, his eyes still wounded. He asks his mother, "Can you bring Asclepius?"

Nyx casts her eyes at Sebastian's body. I don't know what this means. Who is Asclepius?

"Sebastian died defending Iris, defending me," my father says. "He became mortal only to protect your granddaughter."

Nyx floats on the night and hovers over Sebastian. She nods.

"I will summon him."

I look at Aphrodite. She just hushes me. "Wait . . . ," she whispers.

The skies roil, and emerging from the fog is a man in a toga, with a thick, graying blond beard. His face is chiseled, and like Aphrodite and Morpheus—and Nyx and Epiales—his complexion is ageless. I glance at Aphrodite, questioningly.

Aphrodite leans closer to me, and whispers, "He is the god of healing."

Asclepius stares down at Sebastian and intones, "I will heal him, but if the boy has departed with the Ferryman, there will be nothing I can do." He shakes his head. "Such a waste of life, Epiales."

Epiales sulks, arms crossed.

Asclepius unbuttons Sebastian's shirt. He pulls the knife from his chest, then lays his hands on the wound. I hold my breath for what seems like minutes.

Asclepius lifts his hand. The wound has closed as if

it never existed. Sebastian's chest is unmarked. Then Asclepius leans close to him. He inhales and blows—it is as strong as a gale wind.

We all watch—even Epiales—but Sebastian does not move.

Asclepius does it again.

Sebastian lies, still dead. Inside I am wailing, but I want to be quiet, to let this god concentrate. *Please*, I plead the unseen gods of Olympus.

Asclepius leans closer still and blows.

And this time, I can see Sebastian's eyes move behind his lids. He rolls on his side and coughs violently, then inhales in gasps, before sitting up.

"The Ferryman!" he shouts, eyes wide.

"No," Asclepius says calmly. "Not this night, child. Not this night." He offers Epiales a disapproving look.

I sink to my knees and sob in relief.

Nyx rises. "Come, Morpheus. Come, Epiales."

Along with Asclepius, they ascend toward the sky—before I can tell my father I didn't mean what I said. Nyx raises her cloak, shrouding them all with stars.

They blend into the night . . . and are gone.

I kneel beside Sebastian and kiss his forehead.

"You came back to me," I say, through tears.

"Neither the River of Sorrows nor death itself can keep me from you, Iris."

I lean down and kiss him once more. The man of my dreams is here with me again.

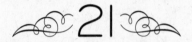

We are such stuff
As dreams are made on, and our little life
Is rounded with a sleep.

WILLIAM SHAKESPEARE, *THE TEMPEST*

My life is so much different now.

For one thing, I sleep. Peacefully. Like normal people. Six or seven hours a night. Though every once in a while, I toss and turn.

For another, my family is a *lot* bigger.

Aphrodite and Nico are expecting a baby. They sold his bakery and her building in Queens and bought a café on Main Street. They serve Greek food and the most *amazing* pastries. People drive from other towns for Nico's baklava after a food critic from the *New York Times* stopped there for a bite to eat and wrote about it. He said Nico was a "baking god." If the critic only knew.

Nico and Aphrodite bought a house on the next block—halfway between Annie's house and ours. I see them every day and can't *wait* to have a baby cousin to spoil. Though I wonder what we will tell the kid about his or her family tree.

Henry Wu and Annie are nauseating. In a good way. He dotes on her. Respects her. He makes her feel like a goddess. And that's a good thing, Aphrodite is always telling us. Never settle, she says. And Annie admires Henry's brilliant brain and loves being treated as if she belongs on Mount Olympus. The funniest thing was when they returned to school as a couple after Christmas break. No one could believe it. Beanpole Henry and one of the hottest girls in the whole school. And nothing thrills Annie more than parading by guys who are jerks, the ones who want to hook up as friends with benefits and then brag about it, the ones who think she is so hot—but there she is with her totally awesome boyfriend.

Uncle Koi is still a hypnotherapist in New Jersey. He comes for Sunday dinners, and he has a new obsession: the Yankees. He and Grandpa go to every home game. He even schedules his patients' appointments around them.

Grandpa is still Grandpa, cash drawer and all.

He bid on a new prize bat, and it hangs above the mantel. He keeps the piece of the old one, I think, to remind us all of what we went through. Like we'd ever forget.

Mom doesn't have Sleeping Beauty syndrome anymore. Not that she ever really did. But she doesn't sleep all the time anymore. It's all still complicated. As part of the deal struck with Hades and Zeus, my father comes to spend one day a week with us. On those nights? Everyone in the world has some ordinary or recurring dream. The missed-connection-at-the-airport or the teeth-falling-out one. Being chased. Or sometimes, he fixes it so that's the night no one remembers their dreams. Anything that doesn't require his full attention.

That first visit after the fight, when he came back to the house, I told him that I just said those horrible things to make Epiales stop. That I really *did* want a father, even if he's not exactly a normal one. As Aphrodite says, normal is overrated anyway. My father understood. He's determined to be a part of my world now, no matter what it takes. We've spent these months getting to know each other. And I'm getting used to having a father around some of the time. He actually took my cell phone from me for a week because I was texting at the dinner table. Which was totally ridiculous, if you ask me, but I kind of like that he cares.

And Sebastian? He lives with Aphrodite and Nico and is excited to be an "uncle" once the baby arrives. Becoming mortal wasn't easy. It wasn't magic. I couldn't do some goddess trick like Nyx and make everything all better. For one thing, school was too hard for him. Trig was bad enough for me, let alone someone who'd never walked in a classroom before. So Henry tutored him, and Sebastian got his GED. Nico and Aphrodite worked with him and trained him. First he was a dishwasher, then a busboy, then a waiter. Nico taught him how to bake and how to make everything on the menu. So now he manages Aphrodite's restaurant—which is called Aphrodite's, of course.

I still feel like the girl in my dreams every time I hear his voice, or hold his hand, or kiss him. He is the man of my dreams. My stomach still does flip-flops. I could kiss him for hours. Just touching him, holding his hand, it all still feels magical to me.

Sometimes, when I go to sleep, I still go down the hallway of many doors. But the hallway is off-limits to Epiales and his kind now. The gods have properly chastised him, and he's stuck in his realm. Hopefully, no new power plays from him for a few centuries.

And when I do dream, when I go down the hallway now, I don't need keys. Sconces *always* light my way. I am always certain of what is behind each door I choose.

After all, I am Iris, the daughter of Morpheus.

And I know my power.

Turn the page to read a
preview of Erica Orloff's
Illuminated!

1

I had another dream... —A.

Like the breath of a ghost against an icy window, the scrawl whispered to us across the centuries.

"Even a book has its secrets. Come on, then, tell us more," Uncle Harry spoke to the manuscript, as if willing it to illuminate. He leaned over its fragile pages like an ancient scholar, staring intently at the parchment.

"Secrets?" I asked him, my voice echoing in the cavernous room of the auction house, its marble floors and twenty-foot-high ceilings carrying even a soft hush like a tree rustling its leaves.

"Callie, everyone, everything, has secrets. Even books. My job is to coax them out." He aimed the ultraviolet light more closely and exhaled audibly.

"What is it?" I whispered, and peered over his shoulder, feeling a tingle like the delicate legs of a spider skittering up my neck and across my shoulders.

He pointed. "In the margin!"

And there, in a spidery scrawl, ethereal words emerged under the bluish light.

"It looks like someone wrote over old hand-writing," I said softly, squinting to make out the words. I knew that as the medieval illuminated manuscripts expert at Manhattan's Royal Auction House, Uncle Harry lived for these parchment books, illustrated by monks, that whispered stories from across the centuries. He talked about them over breakfast and over dinner. He read about them. He wrote about them. Whatever that writing was in the margin, it was the stuff of Uncle Harry's dreams.

"Do you know what this means?"

"Not really."

"It's a palimpsest."

"A what?"

He grinned at me. About six feet tall, with pale blue eyes and dimples, and just the first hints of silver strands in his sandy blond hair, Uncle Harry is the smartest man I know. He has a photographic memory and an encyclopedic knowledge of history. But he's not boring. With him, history is alive.

"A palimpsest! Centuries ago, a *thousand* years ago, paper was rare. So people wrote on papyrus or on goat skin or on vellum. They wrote on parchment and scrolls. Then, when they didn't need that book or information anymore, they washed out the old writing with oat bran and milk or some kind of wash, or sometimes a pumice stone. Then they would write on the parchment or vellum again. And the old writing was lost. They thought forever."

I stared at the feathery script in the margin barely visible in the glow of the bluish ultraviolet light.

"So I'm looking at hidden writing from a thousand years ago? That someone covered over. Secret writing?"

He nodded. "Sometimes we get lucky. The stars align, princess, and you get a gift . . . one of these. They're priceless. Usually time and the elements disintegrate them."

I stared at the book. The strokes in ink were precise, elegant, and each one perfect. No letter was higher than the other—they aligned, no ink blotches, each a work of art. The picture on the page was gilded, the gold not faded by time, and deep blues and greens depicted a knight and a lady, the colors as rich as a peacock's feathers.

"It is beautiful," I said.

"But what makes this even more extraordinary is the hidden writing. Secrets don't stay shrouded forever, Callie. Not really. They always leave a trail, even a thousand years later."

"Did the collector who brought it to the auction house know it was a palimpsest?"

He shook his head. "No. He inherited his father's collection of rare books and manuscripts. The son just wants the cash." Uncle Harry stared wistfully at the manuscript. "Little did he even imagine what secrets were on these pages. The auction for this will go into the hundreds of thousands of dollars, maybe millions. I'll have a better idea once I know more about the manuscript's history." He paused and shook his head. "It's rather sad, really."

"Why?"

"A person spends their whole life amassing a collection of books or antiques. They think it will help them live on forever. And then it gets sold by their kids, who don't really care one way or the other about their parents' stuff. Maybe an obsession can never be shared."

"Maybe. But then . . . here we are," I said. "The words in the margin have lived on. *You* care."

"I still can't believe it. And I know someone else who's going to be elated. I need to go call Dr. Peter Sokolov."

"Who's that?"

"He's a rare-book dealer. The world's foremost expert on medieval manuscripts."

"More of an expert than you? That's hard to believe."

"He was my mentor. And yes, he knows more than even I do. He's someone who understands your crazy old uncle and his love of these ancient papers." Uncle Harry kissed the top of my head. "I told you this was going to be a good summer."

I rolled my eyes. "All right. You found an old manuscript. A *really* old one. One that has secrets. But still I don't think you can count this as a good summer—yet. My father ditched me and took off for Europe with his latest blond girlfriend. Is it me or do they seem to be getting younger and blonder?"

"It's not you. I've never understood your father. Never understood why my sister married him in the first place." Uncle Harry frowned. "I shouldn't have said that."

"Why not? It's true. And as *exciting* as this is, it's, well, a dusty old manuscript." Could I tell him I was hoping for a summer romance? Or an adventure?

"Patience, Callie." He winked at me. "Secrets..."

"What's that supposed to mean?"

"You never know where a secret will take you. It's like playing hide-and-seek throughout history." He said it in a mysterious, yet playfully obnoxious kind of way. "I've got to go make some calls. You can look at the palimpsest. But don't touch it." He walked to his office, and with a backward glance added, "Or breathe on it."

I leaned over and stared at the tiny scrawl that was just barely visible. I squinted. The script was old-fashioned. I couldn't really make out any words.

Then I saw it. At the bottom it was signed.

I had another dream, and this time the sun and moon and eleven stars were bowing down to me.

—A.

2

Touch the stars. Dream of them. —A.

My mother was my palimpsest. She died when I was six, and I've spent my life searching for hidden secrets about her, hoping she would whisper to me the way the scrawl in the margin whispered to Uncle Harry. It's a longing that never goes away. Sometimes, when I see one of my friends hug their mom, I feel an actual ache in my heart. That night, I curled my knees under me and pored over old photos of her when I was alone in my room in Harry's apartment.

My "room"—air quotes there—is what a Manhattan real estate agent calls a second bedroom—meaning it's not much more than an alcove where someone put up a wall. But it has space for me, and it's where I search for my mother's secrets. Uncle Harry has boxes of photos of my mom. He's my mother's brother, and I ask him questions about her all the time. I wonder if I am like her...because I know I'm nothing like my dad.

My father and I have spent our entire lives avoiding each other—in some ways, it's perfect for us that he's never home. During the school year, I lived with my father outside of Boston. Luckily, he travels so much I end up spending half my time with my friend Sofia's family, or being checked on by our neighbor in the condo across the hall. But summers are my favorite time, reserved for Uncle Harry and his partner, Gabe, and New York City. We usually fit in lots of plays, trips to the beach, and once, even a trip to Toronto.

And *this* summer? I was especially grateful to escape. This threatened to be the Summer of the Stepmother, since my dad had been checking out diamond rings with the latest, blondest girlfriend named Sharon. The whole concept kind of made me want to throw up.

After looking at photos of my mom and chatting on Facebook with Sofia, who was spending the summer at a show choir camp, I fell asleep with the TV turned low.

When I woke up, I stared at the ceiling, then looked at the plasma screen on the wall. A morning news anchor with hair perfectly plastered into place was telling me it was six A.M.

"Argh!" I said to Uncle Harry's cat, Aggie, short for Agamemnon. He has one green eye and one yellow, and is a silvery Persian who leaves hair everywhere. "It's summer. I can sleep in. *Why* am I awake?!"

Aggie just meowed and stepped on my stomach before settling down again, purring like a motor. I clicked channels with the remote, too lazy to get up, too awake to fall back to sleep.

About twenty minutes later, Uncle Harry knocked on my door. "You up?" he called.

"Unfortunately."

He poked his head in my room. "What are you wearing to work today?"

I looked over at my tiny closet, which was open and had my clothes spilling onto the floor. "Um...I don't know. Dressy jeans and a sweater set—it's so cold in your office, I'm tempted to wear mittens. And since when do you care what I wear to fetch your coffee? I'm your gopher. I haven't decided. It's too *early* to decide."

"What about this?" He flung a bag from Barney's at me.

I sat up and ruffled a hand through my bedhead mess of curls. I could hear Gabe singing in the shower—"Luck Be a Lady Tonight." He was once in a revival of *Guys and Dolls*. He had played Sky

Masterson. Uncle Harry went to the show twenty times, always sitting in the front row, center seat—which, if you do the math means he spent a small fortune—and he waited afterward with his yellow and black *Playbill* to get Gabe's autograph at the theater door. It's a nauseatingly cute "how we met" story. And the rest, as they say, is history.

It's pretty pathetic when your uncle has a better love story than you've had at this point. Being an affirmed member of the brainy club meant my love life definitely lacked something as adorable. Of course, my grandmother still thinks Uncle Harry just hasn't met the right woman. But at least he knows how to shop.

I peered into the bag, pushed aside the tissue paper, and looked up at Harry. "You're kidding, right?"

I pulled it out and held up the little black summer dress. It was, indeed, adorable. I glanced at the tag.

"*Three hundred and fifty dollars*? Now you've really lost your mind."

"No, I haven't. I've just always wanted to buy an Audrey Hepburn *Breakfast at Tiffany's* dress, but never had anyone to buy one for. Until you! Come on—don't you just *love* it?"

I nodded, shocked. It was probably the classiest thing I had ever owned. "It's gorgeous. Too bad you and a bunch of dusty manuscripts are the only ones to see me in it."

"You can never look too good for a day with goat skin and vellum."

I grinned at him. "Thank you. I really do love it."

After a shower, I let my hair air-dry curly. The weather report said humid—which means there is absolutely no point fighting my hair's true nature. Something that's a cross between a Chia pet and steel wool.

I put on some lip gloss and mascara and a pair of black ballet flats—I also don't fight being five feet three inches. But I'm cheating because really, it's five feet two, and my hair just adds a little height. My skin is naturally pale, with freckles that I also don't bother to fight very much, and I have light gray eyes. I looked over at the built-in bookshelves. Uncle Harry keeps a black-and-white framed photo of my mother. She's looking right at the camera and laughing, her hair blowing in the wind. In the picture, she's wearing this whole Madonna-in-the-'80s outfit, and somehow, she's pulling it off.

I wish I knew what was making her laugh in that picture. Uncle Harry doesn't remember. I look a little like her—different color hair, but the same pale skin. Alas, tanning just leaves me lobster-pinkish.

But I think that's where the similarity ends. Because somehow in every picture of her, she looks like a model, or a bohemian artist, or someone glamorous from a fairy-tale life.

I rechecked my reflection in the full-length mirror on the closet door in my room. I almost looked . . . adult. I smiled back at myself and then stepped out into the narrow hallway. It's lined with posters and Playbills from their favorite Broadway shows—*Guys and Dolls, Contact, 42nd Street, Chicago, Spamalot.* I turned right and walked into their kitchen to make some coffee. It's a big kitchen by Manhattan standards, tiny by Boston standards, with sparkling stainless appliances and gleaming pale maple cabinets and granite countertops. I started toward the coffeemaker.

"No time, sugarplum," Harry said. "Starbucks on the way. We've got to go."

Gabe walked over to me.

"Are you wearing a kimono?" I asked him, fingering the blue and green silk.

"Yup."

"Nice. I'll have to borrow it sometime."

"If I were you, I'd never change out of that to-die-for dress. You look gorgeous."

"Thanks." I stood on tiptoe and kissed him good-bye. "I liked the shower-chorus today."

"You could hear me?"

"Every note."

Harry playfully rolled his eyes. "He's a show-off. He knows darn well we can hear him."

After an elevator ride down forty stories to the lobby and a stop on the corner, Starbucks in hand (I would perish without my coffee—it's life juice), Harry and I walked through jostling morning crowds—but not toward the auction house.

"Where are we going?"

"To Dr. Sokolov's apartment."

"I thought he would come to the auction house so he could see it. Isn't this the kind of find you medieval scholars live for?"

Harry leaned his head back and laughed. "Impossible, I'm afraid."

"Why?"

"He's got agoraphobia."

I tried to remember which phobia that was.

Harry glanced over, "He never leaves his brownstone. *Ever*."

"Ever? Does he work?"

"He does research and writes. He lectures a

satellite class—beamed into the classroom at NYU.
He also does podcasts. Technology is a friend to
people like him. And people bring books to him. Or
in my case, I'll be sending video."

"That's weird. Not leaving the house. How does
he get food?"

"Callie, honey. This is New York. Everything is
delivered."

I thought of the thirty deli, Chinese, Italian, Indian,
and even Ethiopian menus in the junk drawer in the
kitchen. "All right, then, there must be *some* things
he has to leave the house for."

"Maybe. But he has an assistant."

We hailed a yellow cab and about ten white-
knuckle-defying, near-pedestrian-hitting minutes later
stood outside a four-story brownstone down in
Greenwich Village. On either side of the street, trees
stretched toward sky, their leaves arching over the
road, trying to escape their concrete confines. Two
long, sleek black limousines double-parked outside
other brownstones.

"This street is beautiful," I said, climbing out of
the cab. "It's a part of New York that feels secret." I
looked up at Harry.

"That building is where a certain A-list actress

lives. I can't tell you how many times I've been here and spotted Uma Thurman. Oh, and my big crush, Anderson Cooper. Saw him on his bike here once." He nodded toward a three-story brick building across the street. "I think some famous writer lives there. Anyway, Dr. Sokolov is, as they say, old money. His family has owned this brownstone for a hundred years or more. Since back when horses and buggies drove through here. Oh, want a fun, gross fact from history?"

"I'm not sure."

"It has to do with the brownstones. The reason they're multiple stories is so way back when, the rich could live on the top floors away from the stench of horse manure. It was—"

"Stop right there," I groaned. Sometimes, Harry's love of history is just a little too graphic for me.

I looked up and down the street and wondered what it would be like to live there. The street was serene, and I felt transported to another time. I could even hear birds chirping in the trees. I faced Dr. Sokolov's door. A small sign by the bell said SOKOLOV & SONS, ANTIQUARIANS. Harry pressed the doorbell, and it chimed deeply.

The door—fourteen feet high, polished to a sheen,

and probably inches thick—swung back, but instead of some agoraphobic old book expert, I found myself face-to-face with the most gorgeous guy I'd ever seen in my life. I think I turned ten shades of scarlet.

"Hey, Harry." He smiled at my uncle, revealing two deep chasmlike dimples in his cheeks. Then he stared at me. And I thought I felt him stare through me. Or inside me. I took a small step backward and bumped into Uncle Harry.

"Calliope, this is August Sokolov. The esteemed Dr. Sokolov's assistant—and his son."

"Hi," I managed to breathe.

There was a long silence. In that time, I noticed his eyes were green and his brown hair curled a bit at the collar of his shirt. And he had an earring—a yin-and-yang symbol. And a scar in a little horseshoe shape near his left eye. He stared at me. Then he blinked and said, "Come on in. My dad's waiting."

I stepped inside, Uncle Harry behind me. As August led us through a marble-floored foyer, I glared over my shoulder at my uncle as we walked past paintings and even an honest-to-God suit of armor.

What? Uncle Harry mouthed silently, too innocent for words, batting his eyes.

But I kept glaring.

Audrey Hepburn dress, indeed. He was just a little too obvious. He could have warned me, at least.

August ushered us into a huge study with ceilings eighteen feet high. The walls were lined with bookshelves, which in turn were filled with book after book—most of them leather-bound and ancient-looking. A tall ladder with a hook on the top and wheels at its base used to reach the uppermost shelves leaned against the far wall.

A man in a rumpled white shirt sat behind an immense desk surrounded by papers and file folders, silver-rimmed glasses perched on the end of his nose. He stood the minute we walked in, revealing equally wrinkled, coffee-stained khakis. He resembled August, right down to his longish hair and high cheekbones, only older. And messier.

"Harry." He beamed. "Is it true?"

Uncle Harry nodded. "I saw the words myself. So did Callie. My niece. Callie, this is Professor Sokolov."

"Call me Peter."

I said hello and stood by trying not to look at August as Uncle Harry launched into the story of the palimpsest—and soon they were poring over old books. I didn't want to look bored. But really, after twenty-four hours of palimpsest talk, I felt like I could have told the whole story of the manuscript by heart.

August came and leaned close to me. "In about one minute," he whispered, his breath hot on my neck, "they will be so involved talking about their work that they won't notice we've left. Come on, let's go to the garden. I promise to be more interesting."

I glanced at Uncle Harry. He was describing the palimpsest in detail to Professor Sokolov. A bomb could have exploded next to him and he wouldn't have noticed.

I nodded and followed August through the house and out a set of French doors to a garden filled with roses in shades of red, pink, yellow, and a pale purple. In one corner, a small pagoda-style greenhouse stood, its glass fogged from the humidity inside. In another corner an enormous aviary rose skyward.

"Wow," I exhaled.

"Better than medieval manuscript talk, right?"

I nodded. "The manuscript is amazing, though, even if I don't know much about it," I said. "I saw the hidden words."

"My father didn't sleep last night, he was so excited."

"I'm not sure if Harry did, either."

"What about you?" He looked at me playfully.

Was he flirting with me? Guys never did this with brainy girls. I was on track to be valedictorian. My average was a 4.3. I was going to kill Uncle Harry. I tried to think of a snappy comeback, but settled on the very lame, "I slept fine. Well, except for waking up at six when I could have slept in."

"I'm a vampire myself."

"Really?" I smiled at him. "Should I be worried?" *Okay, not a bad line.*

"No. I promise not to bite. But I will stay up all night and sleep all morning. Today was an exception—the palimpsest and all."

"So you know all about them?"

"Yeah. But you don't get to see one often. But I took you out here to escape boring book talk. All right, change of subject. Are you visiting, or do you live in New York?"

"Visiting. I spend every summer here. My dad and I live in Boston. What about you?"

"I was born here. In this house, actually. My mother did this weird bathtub birth."

"Really?" I raised one eyebrow. I was quite positive that if I ever had a baby when I got married, I was going to ask for all the drugs the doctors would give me.

"Yeah. Born in the upstairs bathtub. My mother had two friends chanting, a midwife named Heavenly and my poor dad, who just wanted me born in a regular hospital. So yeah, I took my first breath in this house. Lived here my whole life, just like Dad. I take classes at NYU, work for my dad. He hopes I go into the family business."

"Illuminated manuscripts?"

"Sort of. Manuscripts. First editions. Rare-book dealer."

"The sign said 'and sons.' Do you have brothers?"

He shook his head. "My father is actually the 'and sons.' He and his brother went into the family business—that had been my grandfather's. My uncle died ten years ago. So now it's just my dad. And me. 'And son.' But I really want to be a writer. Write *new* books, not collect old ones."

"But you're his assistant."

He nodded. "For now. I don't know. I love the old books. But not the way he does. My father has his manuscripts. *This* is my passion," August said. He folded his arms across his chest and smiled as he gazed across the gardens. "I write over there." He gestured to a wooden table with a MacBook on it.

"It's beautiful. Did you really plant all this, make this garden?"

"Sort of. My grandmother kept a garden, but it was neglected over the years. I guess I've just brought it back to life. I like being outside. Since my father won't leave the house, I had to sort of make my own vacation spot. Right here."

"Will he at least come out here?"

August shook his head.

I walked to the aviary, which was filled with birds as jewel-colored as the flowers. "They're gorgeous. What kind of birds are they?"

The birds didn't sing so much as titter. One landed on a branch near me, its feathers turquoise, emerald, and ruby-colored.

"They're Gouldian finches," August said. "From Australia."

"But what about those?" I pointed to plain brown ones. They weren't nearly as exotic.

In a quiet voice, he said, "Gouldians aren't usually very good parents. So the society finches step in and raise the hatchlings. They're like finch nannies."

"Sounds like me. I had a nanny until I started high school. And even then, I had to beg not to have one."

August looked at me. "Ah, we have more in common than a palimpsest. Me, too. My Gouldian mother flew the coop when I was ten. Divorced my dad."

"So where's your mother now?"

"California. She couldn't handle Dad's eccentrici-
ties. Or motherhood, for that matter. Bathtub birth
aside, after that, she wanted to 'find herself.'" He did
the air-quote thing.

"And your dad . . . does it bother you . . ." I trailed
off. I didn't want to seem nosy. But *never* leaving the
house?

He shook his head. "He's brilliant, you know. And
that's just how he is. I guess I don't know him any
other way. So I don't miss him being something else.
What about your family?"

I nodded and pointed at a bird with an azure-
crested chest. "My dad is the Gouldian then. My
mom . . . she died when I was in kindergarten. So
it's my uncle Harry who's like that one," I pointed
to a bird preening a baby. "He's the one who takes
care of me. Even when I'm in Boston, we talk almost
every day. We Skype. He flies or takes the train up
every couple of weeks. I come down on weekends
when I can."

I watched the birds dart from nest to nest. "I like
this better than manuscripts. My uncle—you should
have *seen* him when the words showed up in the
margins."